BLAKE
LASER
USS ALTASTARE

HarperAlley is an imprint of HarperCollins Publishers.

Blake Laser

 For information address HarperCollins Children's Books, a division of HarperCollins Publishers, 195 Broadway, New York, NY 10007. www.harperalley.com

Library of Congress Control Number: 2023944814
ISBN 978-0-06-300967-7 — ISBN 978-0-06-300966-0 (pbk.)

Colors by Avery Bacon and Larissa Brown.
Typography by Erica De Chavez Wong 24 25 26 27 28 COS 10 9 8 7 6 5 4 3 2 1 First Edition

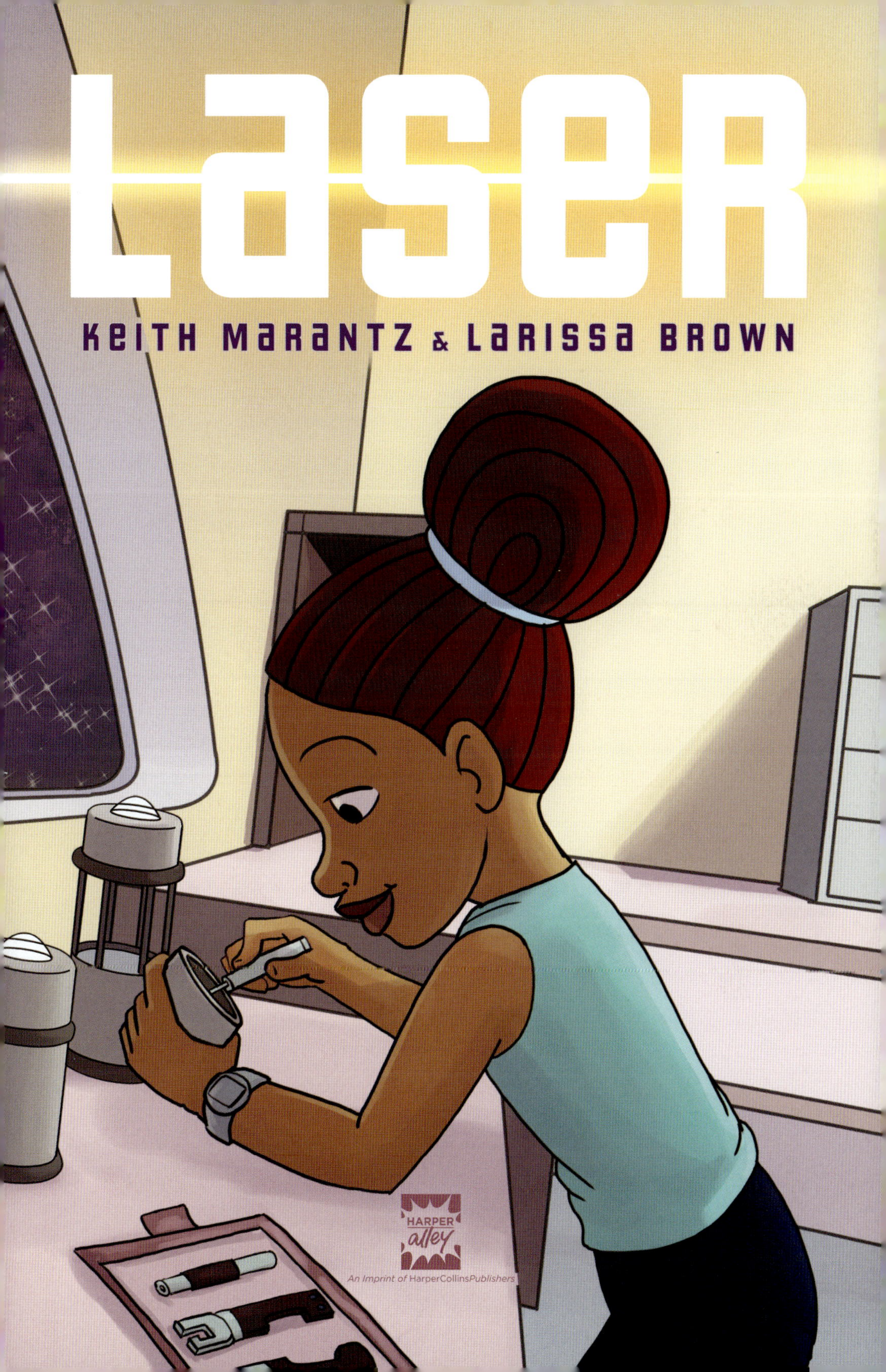
LASER
KEITH MARANTZ & LARISSA BROWN
HARPER alley
An Imprint of HarperCollinsPublishers

CHAPTER 1
MAD SKILLS
2354 A.D.

TATO
PING
DAD STUCK ON BASE. CAN'T COME. ON MY WAY. -MOM
LEVITATO
Come on, come on! Go up. UP! Argh.

Hey, Blake. Why are you yelling at your potato? Won't it levitate?
Oh—hey, Anusha. No luck yet. I'm not sure why it won't work.
So, what's up with nosy over there? Why is he staring at my potato?
I dunno. Maybe he's hungry.
Hee Hee Hee
He's been following me around all night. Like a lost puppy.
A HUNGRY lost puppy.
HA HA HA HA HA

Oooh! SO cool!
I'm Sherman. Sherman Klein. I'll be attending school here next year. Pleased to meet you!
I'm Blake. Blake McClain.
And I don't know yet if I'M pleased.
!
Just kidding. Nice meeting you too.
And this is Anusha Gupta, scientist extraordinaire.
Enchanté.
HEE HEE
heh heh heh
HA HA HA

Quite an impressive design you have here. Great technique. Well executed. It's all so very organized.
Uh, it's okay, I guess—
Does it work? Can I help—
No! Don't touch that!
Okay, sorry! But it IS really COOL. I hope it works.
Thanks. Me too.
I can't wait to do my own award-winning project next year.
Award-winning, huh?
We'll see about that!
heh heh heh
Blake. Move the potato. Let's put him on there!
There is NO way I could get *HIM* to levitate.
Let's try!

Oh, relax. We're just playing with you.
I figured. But let me know if you decide you want help, okay? I have THE MAD SKILLS.
!!
SIGH
Well, good luck with the potato. It's time for a little snowball fight, and I know who my first victim is going to be.
SNOW WONDER
LEVITATO

Too bad it doesn't REALLY snow in New LA. That IS a cool project though.
Fritz DEFINITELY had help from his mom with it.
Speaking of...where are your parents?
My dad is stuck at work. Again.
And my mom is running late.
Oh man, that stinks.
I'm used to it. Have fun in the snow.
If I ever get this thing airborne without another "incident," I'll join you.
You can do it, Blake. You have THE MAD SKILLS.
Whatever. I think the potato's lack of movement would suggest otherwise.
I'll see ya later.

THREE YEARS LATER
Almost got it...
TAP TAP TAP
LOADING
LANGUAGE TRANSLATOR MODULE COMPLETE
Yes!
Success!

Not bad.
Not bad at all.
USS ALTASTARE
SHOOOOOOOOOMM

BEEP! BEEP! BEEP!
incoming transmission
Oh!
New Los Angeles SCIENCE ACADEMY
Hey, Sherman!
Are you Blake McClain, the ASTRONAUT?!
A WHAT? No one uses that word anymore, Sherman.

But, technically, you ARE an astronaut!
I'll read you the definition. Please hold.
astronaut noun
as tro naut
a person who tra yond the earth's atmosphere
Ah! Here we are. "ASTRONAUT. Noun. A person who travels beyond the earth's atmosphere." Yep! That's you, all right.
Then EVERYONE is an astronaut.
We've all done that tons of times— to get to the moon and Mars, you know?
Yeah, but the asteroid belt is REALLY far out! No one goes there. That's so cool.

I guess. So what's up with Anusha?
She's out cold.
She pulled an all-nighter in the lab. We're a bit lost without you here, Blake.
Come on. You guys are geniuses. You don't need me.
Yes, we do. You are the nucleus of our atom.
Without you at the center, we're just helpless little electrons flying aimlessly. It's chaos! CHAOS, I tell you! We need you, Blake. WE NEED OUR NUCLEUS!
Why are you yelling?!

Hey, Sherman, why don't you look up the definition of "NERD."
Hey! Wait. What's a nerd?
Another word no one uses anymore, but I'm hoping it makes a comeback, just for you.
Okay, fine.
Blake, I know it's only been a few weeks since you left, but we already miss you! We can't wait till you get back. A year seems like forever.
Yeah, it does. And being stuck with my family is going to make it seem like a GAZILLION years.
Got it! "NERD. Noun. One strongly devoted to intellectual or academic pursuits, or, a socially inept person."
HA HA HA HA

That sounds like YOU!
HEY!
Okay, guys. I gotta fly. We're having a family meeting. Yay! Say hi to everybody at the academy for me. Miss you!
Bye, Blake!
Love ya lots. Bye, Anusha. Bye, nerd.
ZIIP!

07:55
MEETING IN
5 MINUTES
Where is he?
WHOOSH
SHOOM
BRODY'S
LAIR
ENTER
AT YOUR
OWN RISK
Brody! Wake up!
KNOCK
KNOCK
KNOCK

PULSAR
ZZZZZZZZZZZZZZ

THUMP
THUMP
THUMP
THUMP
BIG BANG

GET! UP! Dad's gonna be mad!
LAIR
THUMP THUMP THUMP
BIG BANG
What time is it?
I'm not your personal alarm clock, Brody. Let's go!
I don't suppose you have a snooze button on you anywhere?
UGH!

YAWN
It's getting a little old always having to wake you up.
Isn't that what little sisters are for?
Humph.
I mean my AMAZING little sister.
ARGH!
HA HA HA HA

Please stop. Save the sucking up for Mom and Dad.
They may buy it, but I don't.
BEEP!
SHOOM
We are here, parental units!

Chapter 2
DIVERTED

Good morning, guys. Right on time! Even Brody! I like it!
Three huzzahs for that, boy.

Oh my!
You're both looking marvelous this morning!
Mother. You're glowing. I didn't know recycled air was so amazing for the skin.
Well, okay then.

It's zero eight hundred hours. Time to start the—
Dad! I know you JUST retired from the military, but can you please be "regular" dad instead of "military" dad and say eight o'clock?
It's zero eight hundred hours and ONE MINUTE.
Daaad!
Blake! Don't interrupt your father!
Don't interrupt your father, Blake!

GRRRRRRRR
Both of you! Stop!
SIGH.
We clearly have an outbreak of cabin fever. I used to see it all the time on missions in the force. Preventing crewmen from blasting each other out the trash jettisons was a full-time job.

It appears that a four-week trip from Earth in tight quarters is wearing everyone a bit thin.
But we fight like this at home.
Let's all take a deep breath.
It's zero eight—
er...it's EIGHT o'clock.
Roughly. Yeah.
Can we get started now?

Okay, Dad.
MCCLAINS' HIDEAWAY
BLIP
Okay, right. So, we are on track to arrive on Asteroid SA22 at one p.m.
This is the perfect place for the McClains' Hideaway. All the distractions of Earth will be millions and millions of miles behind us.
Ooh! We're like astronauts.
Astro-WHATS?
PUNCH
Never mind.
We are lucky to be the first people EVER to build a vacation home on an asteroid.

So we're sort of like the pioneers of the Old West but in space?
Uh—sure, Brody.
YEEHAW!!
What a nebhead.
MCCLAINS' HIDEAWAY
We are so glad we can finally do this as a family. This has been our dream since you were both in diapers.
At least ONE of us is out of diapers.
Child.

MCCLAINS' HIDEAWA
Your mother and I will be boots-deep in planning before the crew's arrival. We'll be very, very busy.
So what else is new?
Brody, we would like you to handle setting up the communications network and entertainment system.
YES!
Can I help you set up the power systems? I like working with circuits too.
Blake, you'll help Brody. He'll let you know what he needs you to do.

What?! No way!
Oh yeah! BOSS BRODY!
So not fair! Why is Brody always the boss?
Blake, did you hear what your mother said? If you have any questions, just ask Brody.
Just ask Boss Brody, Blake.
UGH. It's the twenty-fourth century. Why are brothers still so annoying?

All right then. Touchdown is in four hours. Your mother and I need to prepare the ship for landing, so you two make sure everything in your cabins is stowed. Especially you, Blake, with all your gadgets and little inventions. I didn't realize you were bringing your entire bedroom with you!
I had no idea you had so many toys in there! Your door was always closed.
Mom, they're NOT toys. Plus you hardly ever come in my room so—
INCOMING TRANSMISSION
BEEP BEEP
OFFICIAL TRANSMISSION
INTERPLANETARY SPACE CONTROL CENTER
BLIP

Good morning, Majors.
Good morning, Colonel. What a surprise.
I thought after we retired, we wouldn't have to see your face for a while. To what do we owe the pleasure of your call?
Not good news, I'm afraid. At zero one hundred hours Earth Mean Time today, we discovered that a dense energy field originating from the sun's core is flowing far beyond the reach of our deep-space sensors.
SUN'S
ENERGY
?
72 HRS
The sun is being drained—and fast.
OFFICIAL TRANSMISSION
INTERPLANETARY SPACE CONTROL CENTER

SUN'S ATMOSPHERE ENERGY MEASUREMENT
?
24 HRS
48 HRS
72 HRS
That's not good.
Drained? What do you mean "drained"?
A transgalactic gravitational stream.
It would seem the sun's energy is intentionally being siphoned. At the current burn rate, temperatures will drop so low that in approximately forty-eight hours, Earth will just be a giant ball of ice.
So much for a pleasant family experience.

Like this?
The flow is connected to an unknown signal coming from Asteroid FBX7 in your vicinity. And since yours is the only ship in the sector, we desperately need your help.
I understand the situation, sir, but we're not properly equipped for this mission. Is there anything the control center—
We're too far away. You'll need to work with what you have. We just need you to locate the signal's source and find out everything you can.
Once we know what it is, we may be able to stop the process in time. If not...
life in our solar system is finished.

Well, that's inconvenient.
What? I haven't had breakfast, and all this stress is making me hungry.
CHOMP CHOMP

Well then, Colonel, we'd better make a course correction or we'll miss FBX7. We'll advise upon landing.
Thank you. We'll be awaiting your transmission. And, Majors?
Good luck.

Frank? Can you please reprogram the nav system for Asteroid FBX7? We're almost on top of it.
Right away.
Now, we really don't know who—or what—we're up against here. It may very well be dangerous.
In fact, it could be the most dangerous situation we've EVER encountered. So if we ask you to do something, think of it as an order. You need to listen and do it. Got it?
Got it!
Yes, Mom.

Good. This is going to be a much quicker landing than normal, so the first order is to buckle up and hang on tight.
Course reset for FBX7.
Check.

Hmmm. Scans are showing contact with the tail of Wankel's Comet is imminent.
What??
That can't be right. The comet wasn't expected to pass through here until twenty-one hundred hours Earth Mean Time.
Or was it Jovian Mean Time?
Well, it's here NOW!

BOOM!!
Definitely Jovian! DIVERT!!
What was that?
The wind?
BOOM!!
BOOM!!
Okay, maybe not the wind.
We've lost the portside stabilizer!
Compensating.
We're losing control! Increase portside thrust!
Still compensating.

Got it!
We're stable now. Let's set it down.
Commencing landing sequence.
Brace for landing!
THUD

PHEW!
Welcome to Asteroid FBX7.
Is everyone all right?
Can we go home now?
HISSSSSSS
HISSSSSSS
HISSSSsssSSSsssss!
She sticks the landing and the crowd goes wild!
Ahhhhhh!

All right, that's enough, Brody.
We're all in one piece. No injuries. Great job, hon.
I couldn't have done it without you, hon.
We'd better contact Interplanetary Control.

Shoot! No signal. I don't know if it was the hard landing or all the hits we took, but we're in the dark here for now. It looks like we've got the only horse in this rodeo.
YEE—
Brody!
—haw?
Frank. The signal scanners are functional, and I'm picking up something.
Right. Let's get on it.

Brody, prep Hov-R1 for departure. Make sure the battery is fully charged, and don't forget to pack the charger too.
Aye, aye, Cap'n— er, Major.
Brody, can you handle that?
Uh, yeah. I think so. I mean...
Definitely. No problem.
Can I charge the hov bat? Please?
Oh, Blake. It's so nice you're eager to help, but let's let your older brother handle this.
But I—
Why don't you see if Brody needs anything? We're going to suit up.

YOU NEVER LET ME DO ANYTHING!
GRRR!
Sheesh, where did THAT come from?
She's only twelve.
She'll be fine—though I do wonder if we SHOULD be giving her more responsibility.
She's got some serious smarts for a kid her age. Maybe she can handle more.
She IS smart, but she still has a lot to learn. Maybe after we reconnect more as a family, her attitude will ease up. That's what this trip was supposed to be about.
Well, that's what we were HOPING for, but we've had a sudden change of plans.
Look where we are now.

Chapter 3

I'M IN CHARGE OF THE CHARGE

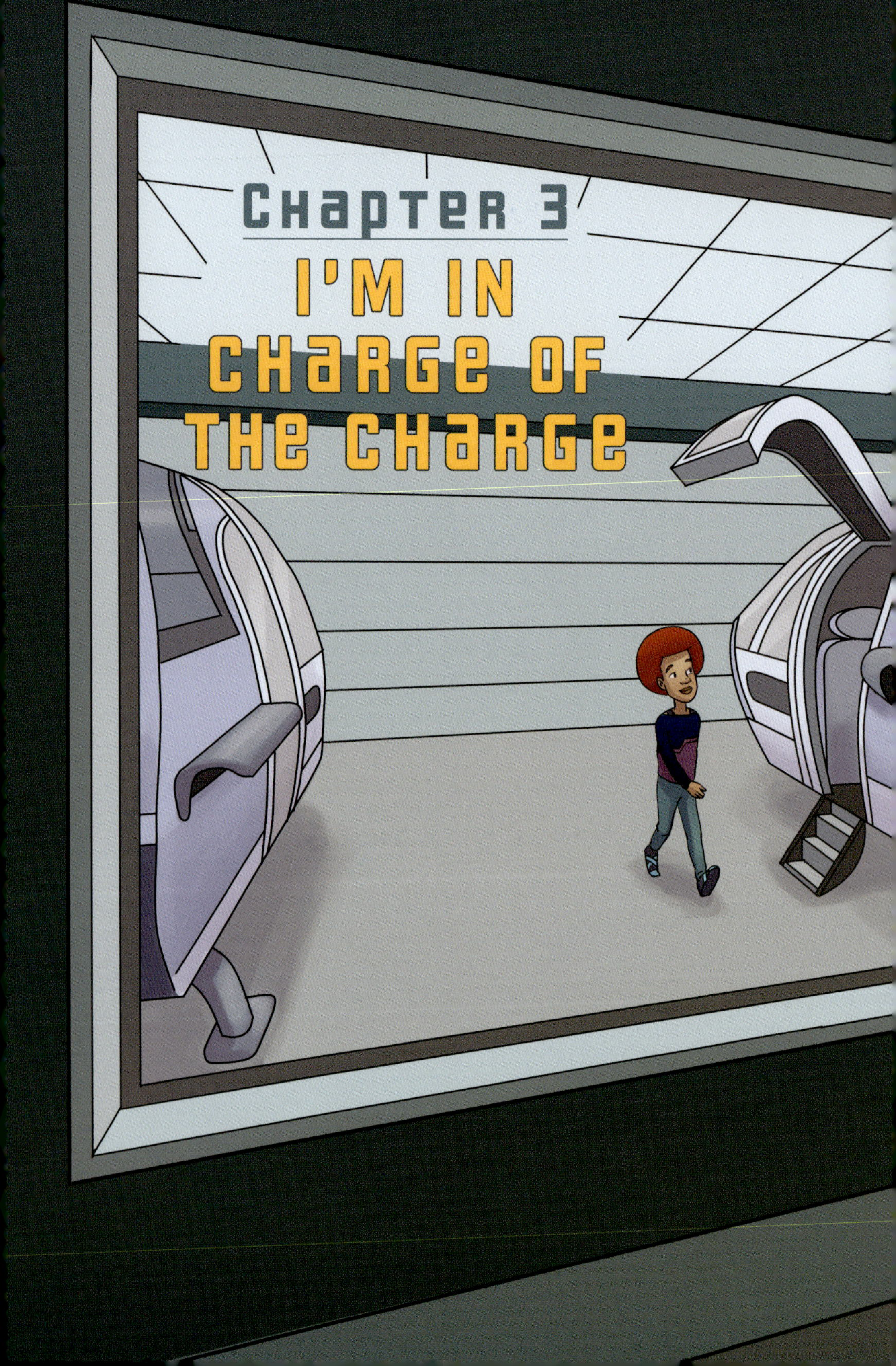

Hmm. What do I do first? Spin it? Turn it? Tap it? Bop it?
CHARGE
Yeowch! Definitely tap it!
CHARGE
HOV BAT CHARGE
WHIRRR

HOV BAT
CHARGE
10
5
HMMMM
VRMMMMMMMMMM
HOV
5
10
HOV-R1
HOV BAT
CHARGE LEVEL
100%
CRACKLE
FIZZZZZT
Whoa! What a rush!
WHOOSH
Why does it smell like something is burning in here? You're supposed to be charging the hov bat!

Check it out, Blake! You have to do this! Once you get to six, everything starts to get all tingly. Try!
What are you, five years old right now? Quit messin' around.
Relax. It's aaaall done. I cranked it to the max. Really fast, like, zip, zap, done!
You just cranked it? That's not how to do it.
You're supposed to increase the charge gradually, you neb. And there was no pulse?
I have a pulse.
No, Fizzbrain. An electromagnetic pulse. From surging the charger. You could have fried something in here. Any uninsulated equipment or exposed circuitry is vulnerable.
Ohhh! Well, there may have been a teensy-weensy pulse, but it's all good now. They're ready to roll, er, uh, hover.

HOV-R1
HOV BAT
CHARGE LEVEL
100%
Uh, Brody? This charge doesn't look stable. It could discharge too quickly. I think we should discharge it and start over.
Nah. It'll be okay. Besides, they're in a hurry. Time is short and so are you.
I don't know, Brody. I don't think this is a good—
It's FINE.
Now this calls for the EXTRA-STRENGTH anti-antigravity cream.

Why isn't she here yet??
Since you didn't come to the snow, the snow is coming to you.
Oh, thanks.
Any luck yet? Have your parents showed up?
Nope, and... nope.
This tastes JUST like REAL snow! Yum!
MMM. So good!
It's just frozen water, you know.

Aww!
Okay, back to the snow! Blake, meet us when you can, okay? You've got this.
PLOP!
Yeah, yeah.
Hm...
What's wrong, my little prodigy?
Oh, hi, Dr. M. I can't get my potato to cooperate. It was working fine the other day...until it blew up.
And my mom is running late.
Well, perhaps your fear of failing may be keeping you from seeing things clearly.
A great woman once said, "You gain strength, courage, and confidence by every experience in which you really stop to look fear in the face. You must do the thing you think you cannot do." Do you know who said that?
MATERIALS
DATA
Eleanor Roosevelt, over four hundred years ago.

And here's another one for you. "Emotions will never stop you from doing anything unless you let them. In your quest for success, they can either be your enemy or your ally. The choice is yours."
That was spoken by a wise woman not too long ago.
VITATO
Who said that?
I did.
It looks like you're on the right track. I know you can do this, Blake.
Thank you, Dr. M.!
Blake?

Blake? How is everything going? Did Brody take care of the hover?
Uh... yeaaah. Yeah, he did.
Great!
Hon? Could you give me a hand with these snaps? I could have sworn this suit fit better when we left Earth. Maybe it's from the lack of exercise out here.
Maybe it's from the lack of self-control. You have been hitting that freeze-dried cookie dough pretty hard since we left.
Cuz they're so good! You know, we didn't have these in the Force unless we smuggled them in. Most mess officers weren't big on sweet snacks.
SPACE DOUGH
Sugar and young cadets can be an explosive combination.
Really? Now? If you keep eating those, you're gonna split in two!
I missed them! But I missed your cooking more. Well, except for your roasted okra. That, not so much.
Maybe if you were eating more roasted okra out here, you wouldn't need my help stuffing you into that suit.
Ouch. Good point.
But there was something much more important I missed while being gone so long.
We missed you too, Dad.

And here we are leaving you again. Will you two be okay while we're both gone?
We'll be fine.
You're bringing blasters?
Well, something or SOMEONE is responsible for that signal. Let's just hope they're friendly.
So, we're good to go, then?
Uh—
Uh, what?
Nothing. Yeah. It's ready.
Keep your coms live at all times. That's mandatory protocol when a team is off ship. We'll be back soon.
Okay, Mom.
Now go clean your room.

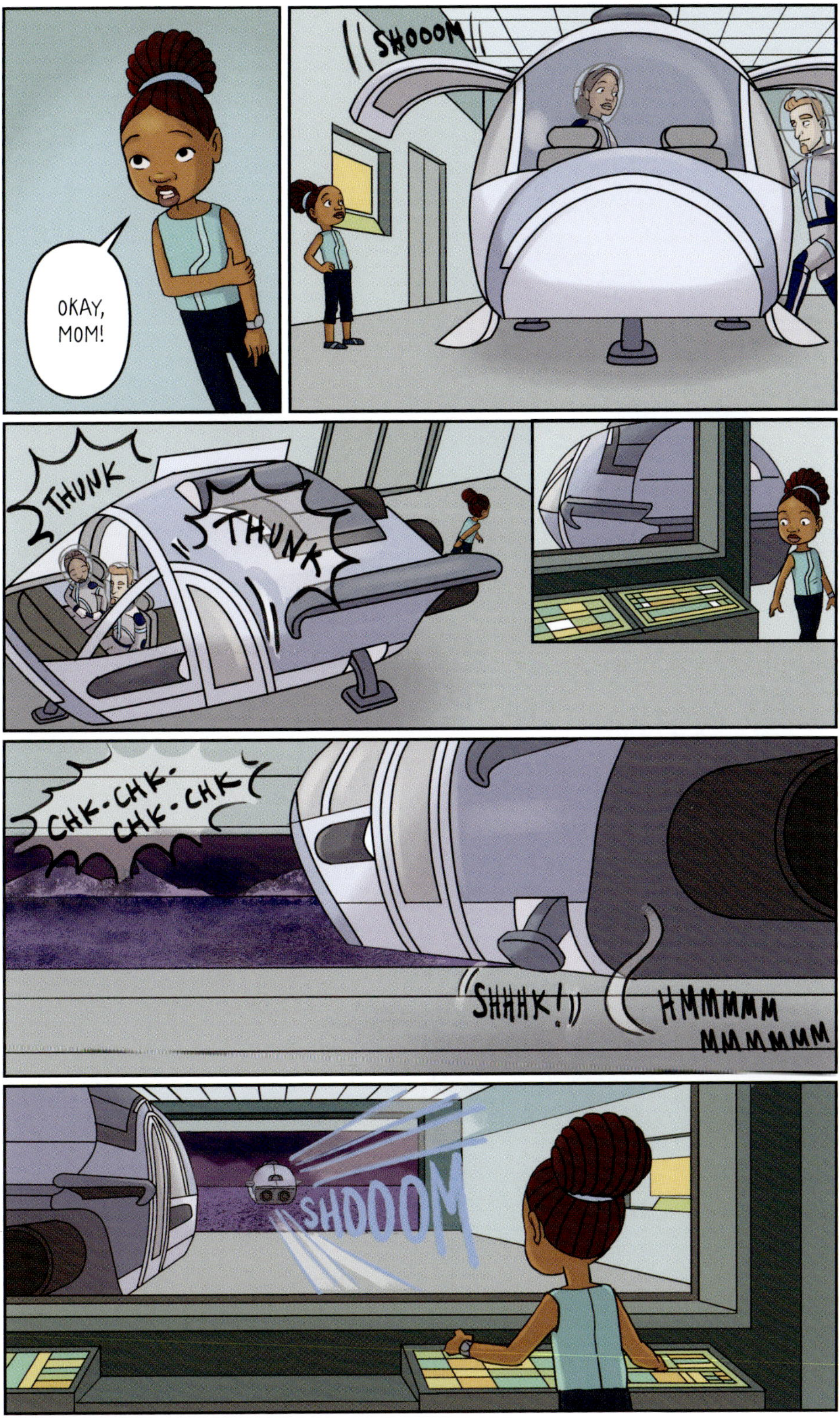
OKAY, MOM!
SHOOOM
THUNK
THUNK
CHK-CHK-CHK-CHK
SHHHK!
HMMMMMMMMMMMM
SHOOOM

Now, where'd I put...?
LOCATE PAD
BEEP BEEP
BEE BOP SKIDDLY BEE BOP!
IT'S NOOGIE TIME!

Hey! What are you doing up there? Get off me!
Yeah—time for YOUR noogie!
HOLOGRAM OFF
ZIP

Hey! How did you do that?
Neat trick, huh? That's my holo projector module. Just a little something I cooked up.
Whoa! Your holo pad. That's not standard issue.
Oh, it is. I just... gave it a little love.
And my watch too.
I don't know what comes after next-level, but whatever level that level is, that's the level those are on!
It's not that big of a deal, really. It didn't take me that long.
WHOA! What's that?
It's just a lamp. Well, technically, it's a quantum laser light magnifier. It excites quantum-sized particles in the orb laser and emits exponentially magnified light and energy.
So it's a FANCY lamp.
BRIGHT LIGHT! BRIGHT LIGHT!
That's the source for the—
Got a laser blaster? Pew! Pew!
Well, I made these things that sort of, uh— They're not REALLY blasters but, uh—

Can I have one?
Uh, no.
Pretty please?
No.
Aww.
Oooooh, must touch.
DON'T!
OUCH!
OUCH! Zagbar? Why did you hit me?
You're not paying attention to the monitor, Karl. There's an alert! That little thing is flashing and you're not doing anything about it!
Would you look at that! The system has detected another source of energy output on the asteroid...not too far from here. I wonder what could be causing it?

Zagbar, there's not supposed to be any life in this star system, right?
That's what we were told, yeah.
Well, there's SOMETHING here besides us.
Should I have the sentries go check it out?
Nah, just alert the scouting team and let them handle it. It'll give them something to do.
Owie!
Yeah, it's hot.
Vewwy hot.
Well, don't touch my laser, Mister Touchy-Pants.

"Don't touch my laser. Never touch the laser."
"It's Blake's laser! It's—"
Heyyy! Blake LASER.
Under the authority given to me, by me, FOR me—I proclaim that forthwith, henceforth, and withforth—
that forevermore, you shall be known as—
BLAKE LASER!
BLAKE LASER. Hmmm. I like it!
Blake Laser and Boss Brody!
No!

Wanna see this fancy lamp in action?
Pretty cool, right?
I wouldn't have been able to come up with that in a million years. You're too smart, Blake Laser.
Have you showed Mom or Dad?
Well, they always seem busy, so I figure there's no point.
I bet Mom couldn't even figure out how half these things work. You have some insane stuff going on here, Blake. Seriously, you could change the world.
No. You heard what Mom called them. TOYS.
Besides, with the sun's energy being siphoned, there may no longer be a world to change soon anyway.

Whoosh. That's dark. You're depressing me now.
Well, it's true.
Ah, Mom and Dad got this. Want a chocolate?
Uh, no thanks. I'm not like you. When I'm stressed, I CAN'T eat.
Well, if you change your mind, I'll save a Big Bang Bar for you.

INCOMING TRANSMISSION
BATTERY ALMOST DEAD. BRODY BRING CHARGER. BLAKE STAY ON SHIP. NEAR ICE POO
Ice poo? What's ice poo?
Let me see.
The transmission was cut off! Their battery must have died! See?! I told you! And why don't they have a charger? Brody, did you not pack a charger?
Uh—
Did you even read the Operations Checklist for the HOV-R1?
Uh, sort of?
READ THIS CHECKLIST CAREFULLY
The first line says in all caps, "READ THIS CHECKLIST CAREFULLY"!
Well, I read THAT line carefully.
BRODY!

This is bad. It's my fault.
No. It's mine.
I knew you made a mistake and I didn't speak up.
SHOOM
We need to prep HOV-R2 for you ASAP.
For ME? Aren't you coming?
Uh, no. You read the message. It's protocol that I stay on the ship. You'll be fine.
The heck with protocol! This is no time to start throwing protocol around. We already have Mom for that.
I can't leave the ship unattended. Mom and Dad would freak out! I have to stay here.
Sorry, Brody. You'll be fine.
I can't do this on my own. Please, Blake?
SIGH. Ugh! Fine. Let's go. And don't forget the chargers!
SHOOOM

Chapter 4
ZAP!

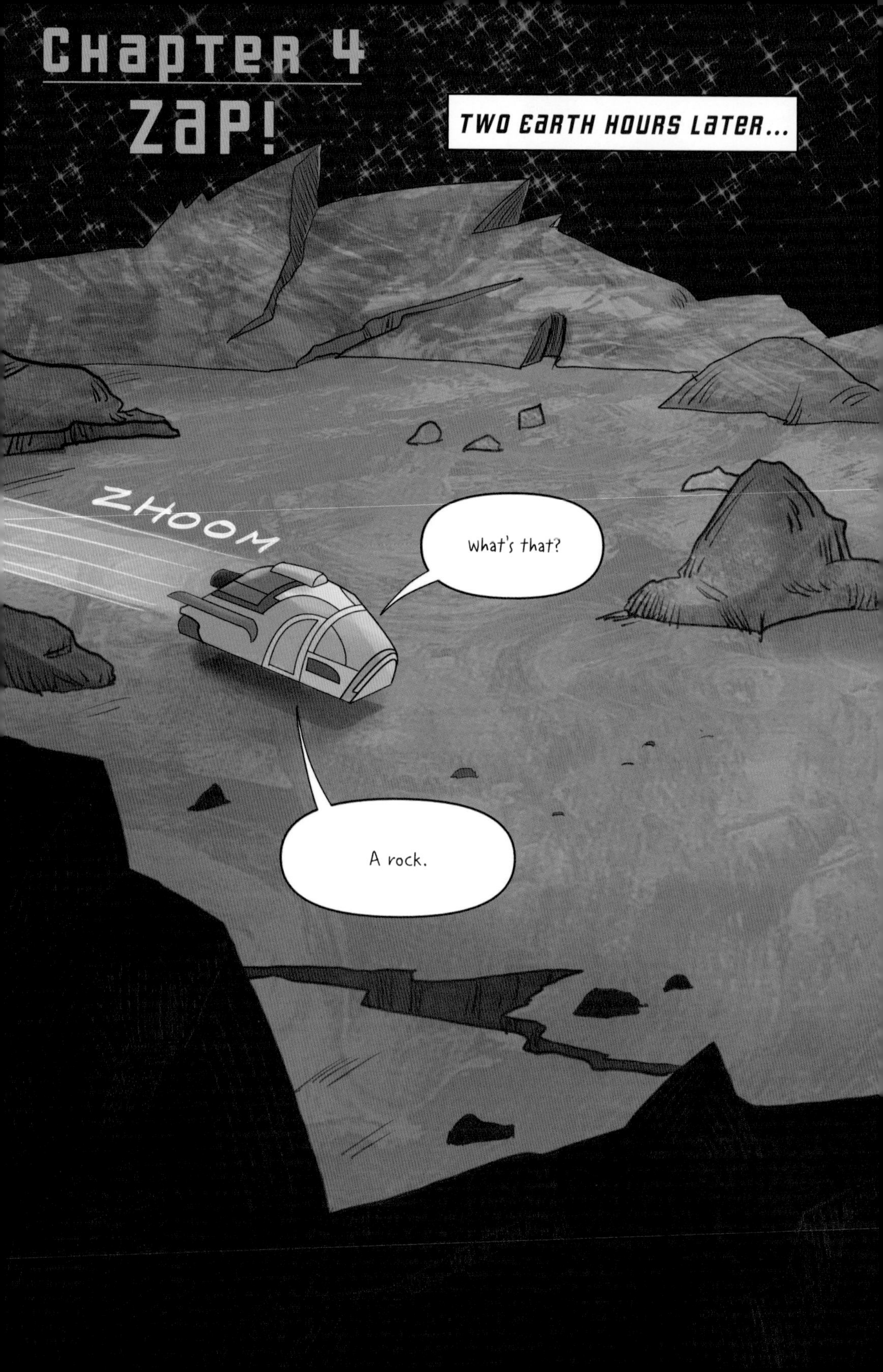
TWO EARTH HOURS LATER...
ZHOOM
What's that?
A rock.

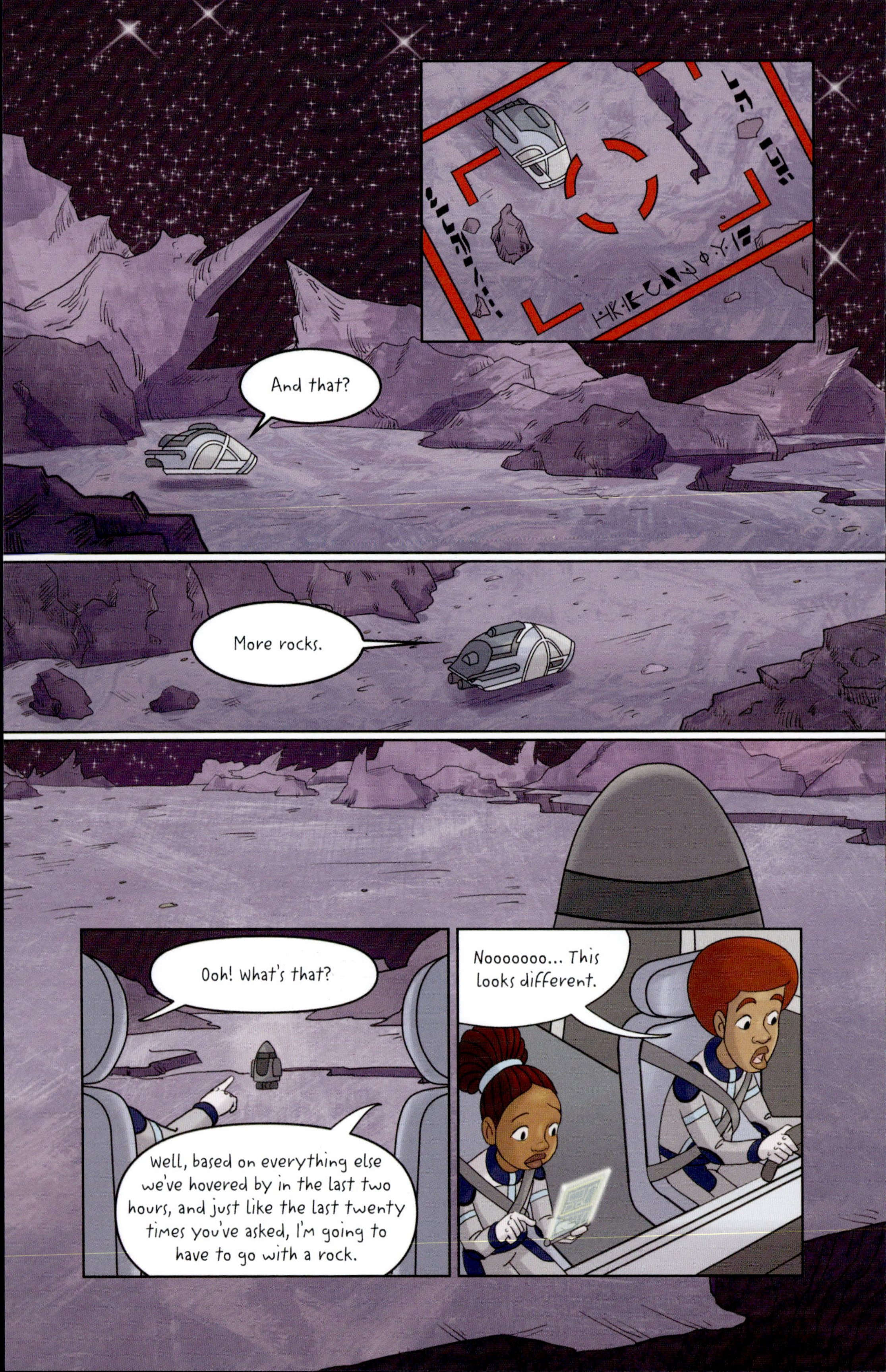
And that?
More rocks.
Ooh! What's that?
Well, based on everything else we've hovered by in the last two hours, and just like the last twenty times you've asked, I'm going to have to go with a rock.
Nooooooo... This looks different.

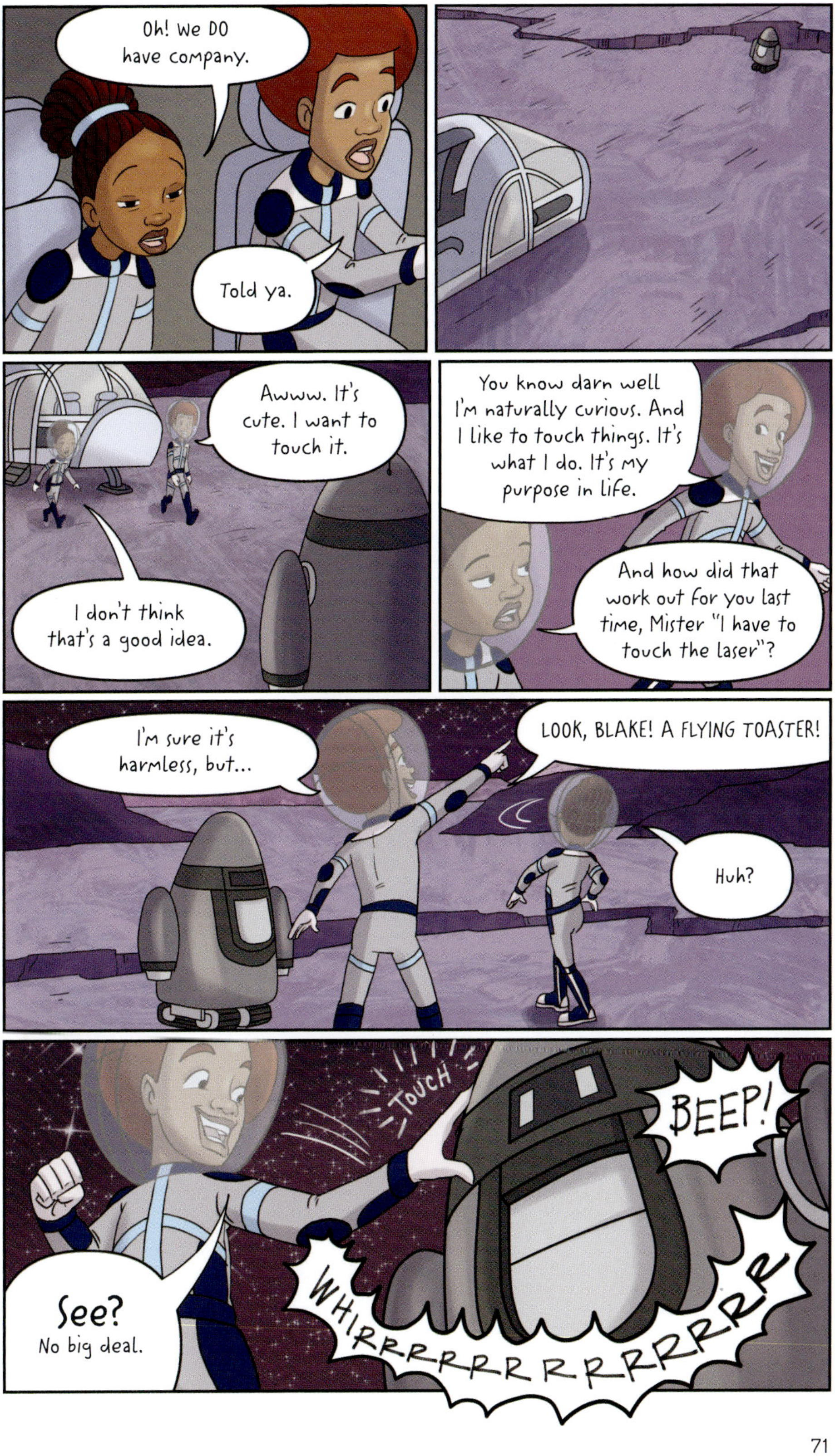

Oh! We DO have company.
Told ya.
Awww. It's cute. I want to touch it.
I don't think that's a good idea.
You know darn well I'm naturally curious. And I like to touch things. It's what I do. It's my purpose in life.
And how did that work out for you last time, Mister "I have to touch the laser"?
I'm sure it's harmless, but...
LOOK, BLAKE! A FLYING TOASTER!
Huh?
TOUCH
BEEP!
See? No big deal.
WHIRRRRRRRRRRRRRRR

BRODY!
SCREEEEEEEEEECHH
SPIT
SPINNNNN
WHIRRR
SPIT
SPIT
SPIT
SPIT
HOV-R2
Where'd all those bugs go?

TAP
TAP TAP
TAP TAP
HOV-R2
ZAP
ZAP
ZAP
OUTER AIR SEAL BREACHED
What do we do now?
I don't know!
INTERMEDIATE AIR SEAL BREACHED
Wait just a sec.

I'm picking up a signal coming from the big guy. It looks like he's sending commands to them.
You mean he's the boss—like me?
Yeah, about that boss thing...
WARNING CABIN SEAL FAILURE IMMINENT
Blake, our shields!
SHOOM
SHOOM
OVERRIDE SYSTEM
ENTER COMMAND
Let's see how his friends like these new commands—
TAP TAP TAP
—compliments of Blake Laser.

WHOOSH
SEND COMMAND
Bon voyage!
SCRIT
SCRIT
SCRIT
SCRIT
SCRIT
SCRIT
SCRIT
SCRIT
SCRIT
SCRIT
Yes!

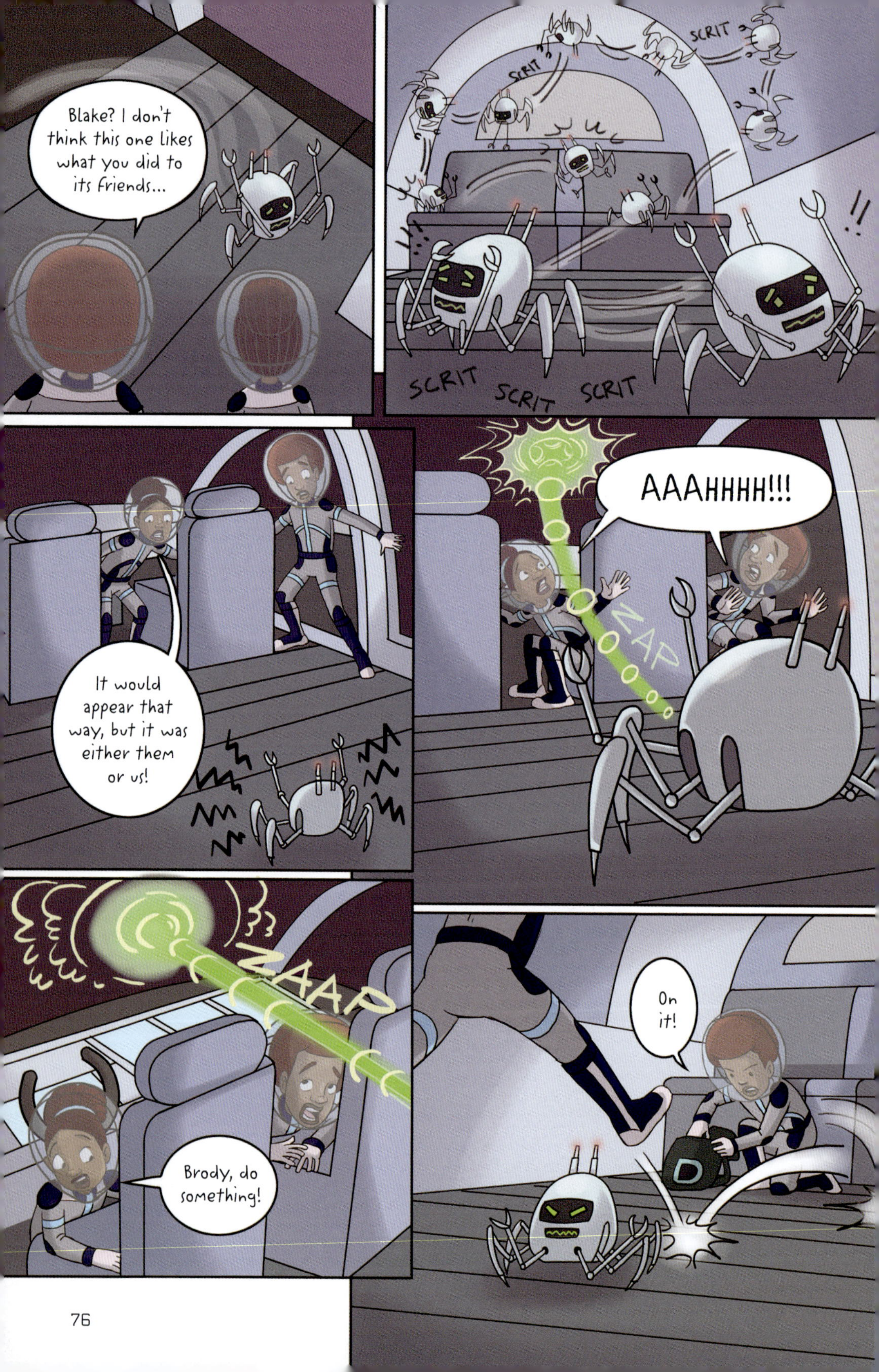
Blake? I don't think this one likes what you did to its friends...
SCRIT
SCRIT
SCRIT
SCRIT SCRIT SCRIT
It would appear that way, but it was either them or us!
AAAHHHH!!!
ZAP
ZAAP
Brody, do something!
On it!

CLINK
SCRIT SCRIT
Come back here so I can squish ya!
SCRIT
SCRIT
SCRIT
SCRIT
SHOOP
SHOOM
You just HAD to touch it, didn't you?

BOOM
GET DOWN!
BOOM
What WERE those things?
I don't know, but I hope they don't come back.
We'd better check for damage.
Do you know how to read any of these instruments?
Yeah— and it looks like one of the power converters is fried.
Now what?
Let's try to contact Mom and Dad. We might be close enough to pick up their com units by now.
Huh? I'm picking up an audio signal, but it's not theirs. Listen!

Is that French?
Definitely not French.
What is it?
LANGUAGE UNKNOWN
I don't know, but I should be able to translate it.
How?
I built a module that can translate any language or learn a new language once it has enough data to process.
LANGUAGE LEARNING
Heha kuwi wasa, Zagbar.
SUCCESS
NEW LANGUAGE LEARNED
TRANSLATION TO ENGLISH
"CHECK THIS OUT, ZAGBAR"

What's a Zagbar? They're still talking. Keep translating!
Nina nini kuli hapa?
REAL TIME TRANSLATION
I wonder how long this one's going to last?
I don't think it's going to last very long at all. What do you think, Za—
What happened? What's not going to last?
I dunno. Argh. It stopped working.
Can you fix it?
I don't know. Lemme see. It's gonna be a minute.
I mean, look at it. It's so small! And it's not very hot at all.
You're probably right. It does look like we'll need another star sooner rather than later.
I'm getting sick of bouncing from one star system to another. But it's all for the greater good, I suppose.
Charging old stars like ours isn't easy. It's a good thing we have the Borsulons for that.

It's working now!
What did we miss??
We do plenty for the Borsulons. They've already got us mining our own crystals on Mutalon 5 for their use.
We should be grateful. It's their technology that has kept our planet alive this long and made our lives better.
You really believe everything the Borsulons say, don't you?
It's true, Zagbar!
Whatever you say, Karl. Now get back to—
TRANSMISSION LOST
Borsulons? Mutalon 5? What are they talking about? Did we just discover that aliens exist?
I don't know, but that Zagbar guy sounds like a jerk!
I hope he's not as bad as our robot friends.
Let's fix this ship so we can get to Mom and Dad before anyone—or anyTHING—else does.

Chapter 5

THE ALIEN AGENDA

Uh, Zagbar? The energy level looks like it's dropping even faster now.
We'd better contact the Borsulons. Get Krutahna on the screen. Flart will want a report before his arrival.
BEEP
What is it?
BLIP
Hello, madam. We're checking in on behalf of Ultimate Supreme Flart. Any idea how much time we have left with this current star?

Not long. Not long at all. That I can tell you. It's WAY too small for your needs.
Too small?
It was a huge mistake.
My new assistant is as dumb as a two-headed florox. I'll need to put in another request for a new star. And please do have Flart contact me as soon as possible. Got it, Zagbag?
It's Zagbar.
How long will it take to find one?
I have no idea, Zagbag. I'm already up to my neck stalk in orders. Mutalon 5 isn't the only planet that needs something from Borsulon, Inc., you know.
Now listen to me, Krutahna...
Look, we *should* have a new star located before this one goes fizzle fizzle. Hopefully. Okay, Zagnut?
It's ZAG—
ZIP

Ugh. I hate it when she hangs up on me.
"Hopefully"? What did she mean by "hopefully"?
Ah, relax. Don't listen to her. They need us as much as we need them. If we're gone, they have no one to mine the planet. She's just trying to assert her superiority by instilling fear in us.
THUNK!!
It worked. I'm full of fear and feeling quite inferior, thank you very much.
We need to tell Ultimate Supreme Flart right away!
Oh, we can't tell him yet. He'll blow a gasket. Let's just tell him what he wants to hear and we'll fix it before he arrives. And why can't you just call him Flart?
YOU can just call him Flart because he's your dad. If I just call him Flart, it's mind-control prison for me. No thank you.

Now, about this other problem...
See that pretty blue one? Scans are showing that there ARE some complex life-forms there! They're all going to die when their star fizzles out.
Ah, who cares. They're probably not half as complex as us. I'm sure they won't even know what's happening to them.

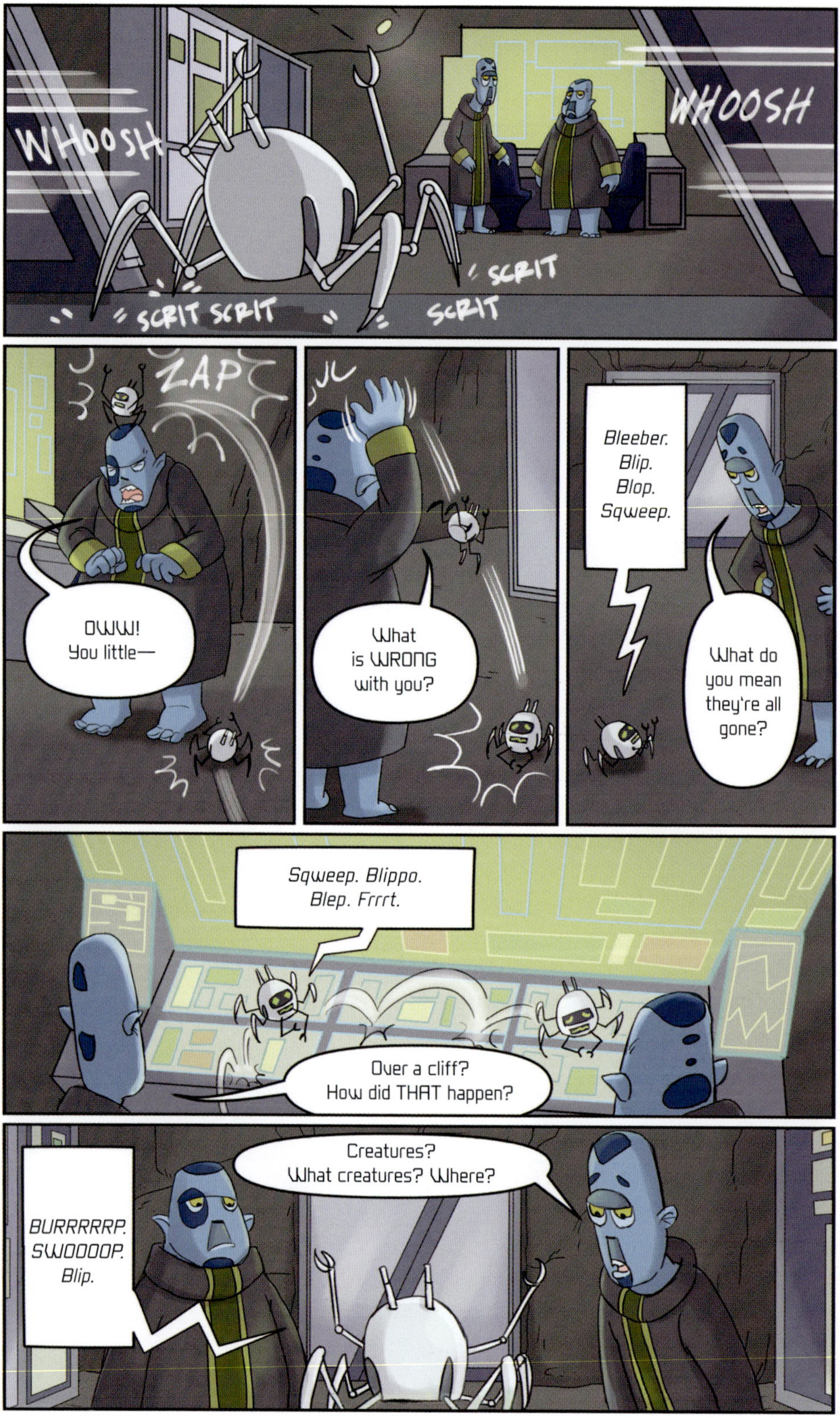
WHOOSH
WHOOSH
SCRIT SCRIT
SCRIT
SCRIT
ZAP
OWW! You little—
What is WRONG with you?
Bleeber. Blip. Blop. Sqweep.
What do you mean they're all gone?
Sqweep. Blippo. Blep. Frrrt.
Over a cliff? How did THAT happen?
BURRRRRP. SWOOOOP. Blip.
Creatures? What creatures? Where?

Murrg. Vleedo. Frrrp?
Yes, we will get you more friends.
Eeeep. Toosh. HAAP!
SCRIT
SCRIT
Yes, we'll find whoever did this—and they will answer to us. The security team will see to that.
BZZZRTT!

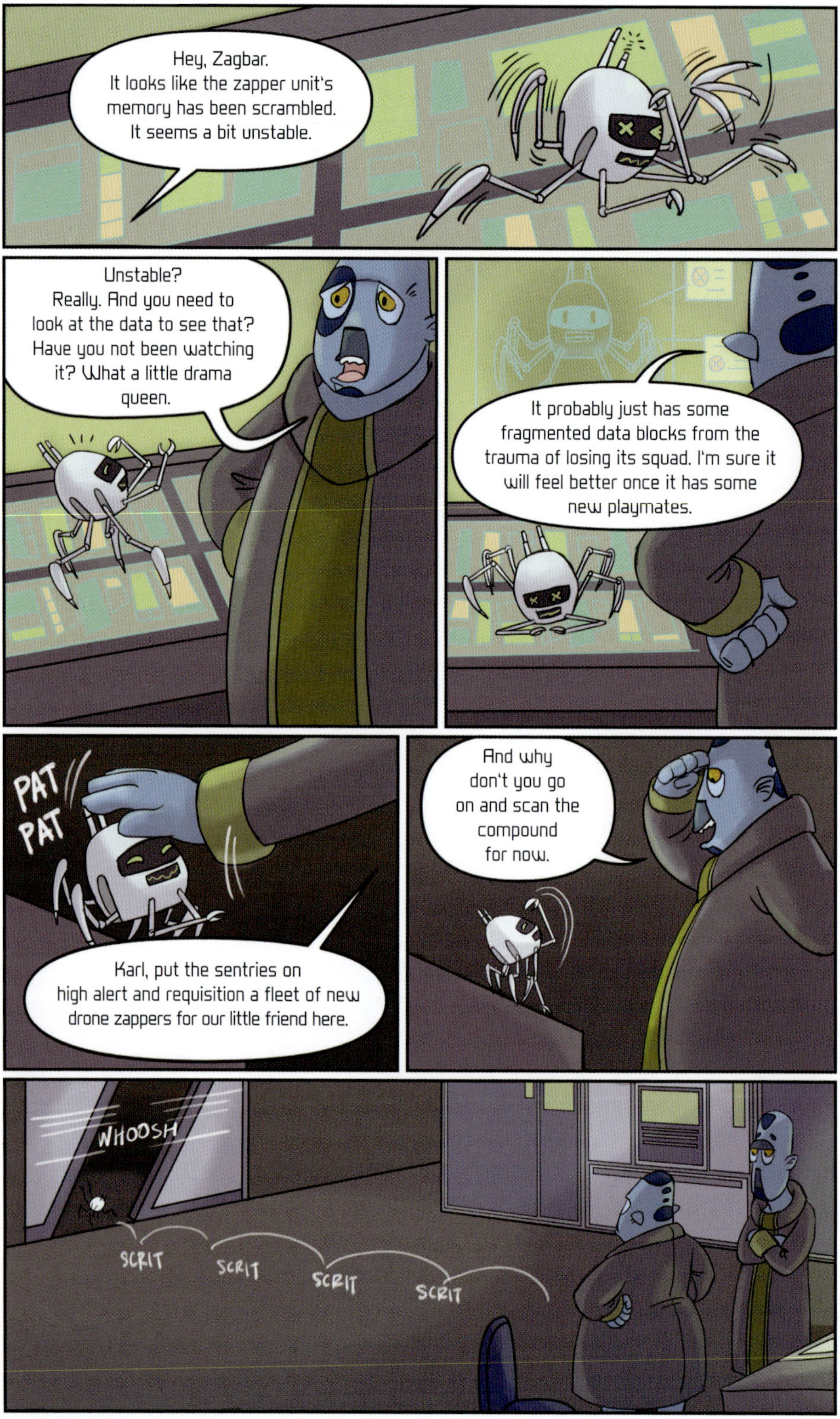

Hey, Zagbar. It looks like the zapper unit's memory has been scrambled. It seems a bit unstable.
Unstable? Really. And you need to look at the data to see that? Have you not been watching it? What a little drama queen.
It probably just has some fragmented data blocks from the trauma of losing its squad. I'm sure it will feel better once it has some new playmates.
PAT PAT
Karl, put the sentries on high alert and requisition a fleet of new drone zappers for our little friend here.
And why don't you go on and scan the compound for now.
WHOOSH
SCRIT
SCRIT
SCRIT
SCRIT

The sentries and the new drone zappers, Karl! Get on it!
Why do I always have to do everything? I don't like it.
Because I'm your superior.
Yeah, but it's only because you're the son of the Ultimate Supreme Flart.
Trust me. I don't like that either. Now do it!
REACH
BEEP!
There. Happy now? It wouldn't kill you to press one lousy button, would it?
You press the buttons, Karl. Not me.
HUMPH.

Whatever, Zagbar—but I REALLY think we should tell Ultimate Supreme Flart about all this.
BLIP!
Tell Flart what?
You left the audio channel open! Again!

You'd better have good news for me.
Uh, I do! It's going well, Dad.
Listen, I appreciate you coming all the way from Mutalon 5 to check on this operation, but everything is fine. You'll see when you arrive.
It better be. You know I don't like to be disappointed.
Oh, I know. I KNOW.
Well, good. Now, back to my nap. I'm not even there yet and I already have warp lag like you wouldn't believe. Tell me when you hear from Krutahna. Flart out.
We should have told him.
No way.
BLIP!
As soon as Krutahna gets back to us with the location of our new star, THEN we'll tell him.
As for now, we have some intruders to take care of...before they cause any more problems.

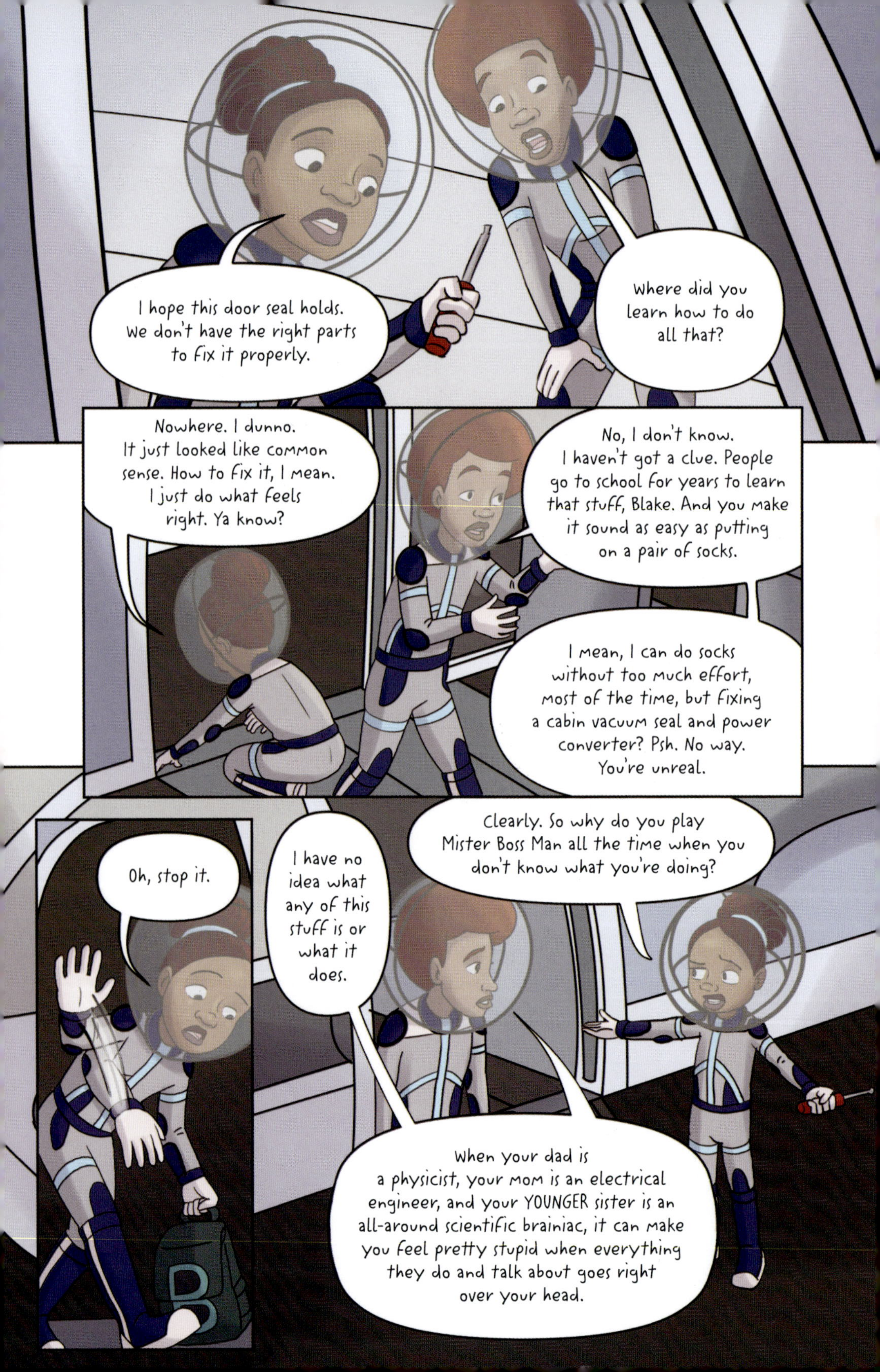
I hope this door seal holds. We don't have the right parts to fix it properly.
Where did you learn how to do all that?
Nowhere. I dunno. It just looked like common sense. How to fix it, I mean. I just do what feels right. Ya know?
No, I don't know. I haven't got a clue. People go to school for years to learn that stuff, Blake. And you make it sound as easy as putting on a pair of socks.
I mean, I can do socks without too much effort, most of the time, but fixing a cabin vacuum seal and power converter? Psh. No way. You're unreal.
Oh, stop it.
I have no idea what any of this stuff is or what it does.
Clearly. So why do you play Mister Boss Man all the time when you don't know what you're doing?
When your dad is a physicist, your mom is an electrical engineer, and your YOUNGER sister is an all-around scientific brainiac, it can make you feel pretty stupid when everything they do and talk about goes right over your head.

Don't say that. You have plenty of talent. I could never draw like you do.
But what good is my AMAZING artistic ability going to do for us here?
Look, if we're going to get out of this mess, we need to work together. As a team. Okay?
Okay.
Yikes! It's getting really cold!
It's getting really cold!
Hey, look! It's actually SNOWING!
It's not supposed to snow in New LA! The odds of that happening are astronomical!
So is getting hit by lightning. I'm going back inside.

Chapter 6
Ice Poo

So where do you think the ice poo is?
I don't think that's what we're looking for, Brody. We need to figure out what they were trying to say before their battery died.
RATTLE RATTLE RATTLE
WARNING CABIN SEAL FAILURE
I knew the seal patch wouldn't last long, but I hoped it would last longer than this!
SHIELDS!
RATTLE RATTLE
SHOOM
SHOOM
FWOOM

Slow down!
RATTLE RATTLE
SHHHHHHMMMM
ICE POOL!
They were trying to say ice pool!
You're right!
Phew!
I didn't want to have to deal with any ice poo.

Go...GO!
KIDS!
MOM!
DAD!

I'm so glad you found us. We had just located the signal and were getting ready to investigate when the battery started to fail.
Blake? What are you doing out here? You were supposed to stay on the ship.
I'm just trying to help.
It's my fault. I made her come with me. And if it wasn't for her, we wouldn't have been able to find you. Not a chance.
Well, it's good you're both here. Now, let's get the hov bat charged on HOV-R1.
We're also going to need to fix HOV-R2. I did my best with the repairs after we were shot at, but...

Shot at?
By who?
Robots.
Robots?
ALIEN ROBOTS!
This is not a good time for your jokes, Brody.
No! He's serious! After we were attacked, we picked up a transmission that I translated, and they were ALIENS!
Translated how?
With the translator I made.
Okay, enough with the fooling around. Let's get our hover charged up and swing around to the other side of those rock formations. That's where the signal is coming from.
Done. The battery is charged. Let's go.
HDV-R1

SHOOM
WHHHIIIIRRRRRRRRRR
RRRHHHHHMMMMM
Why aren't we moving?
The hover has been sitting here for so long, it's frozen in place. The lift units don't have enough thrust to break free.
HOV-R1

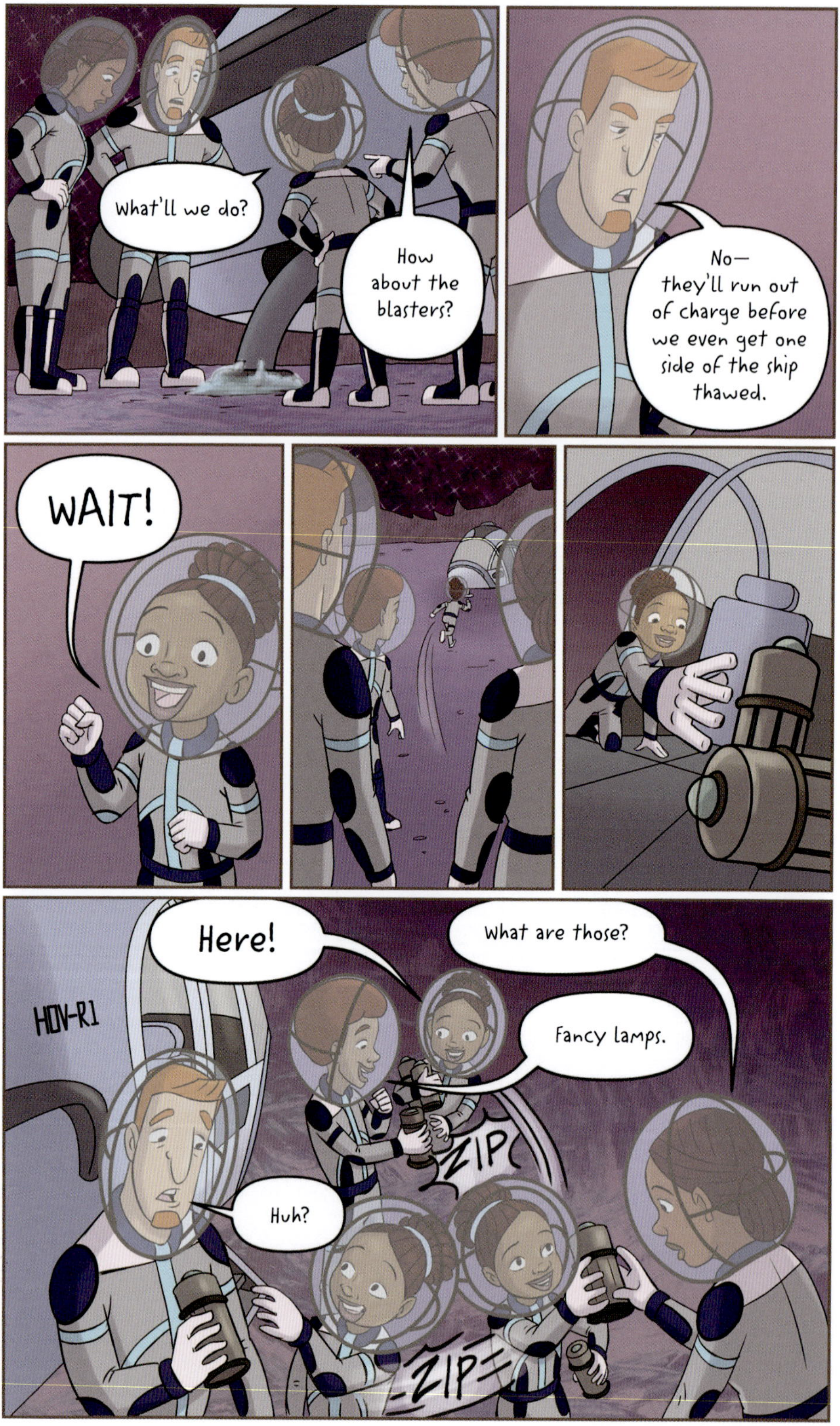
What'll we do?
How about the blasters?
No— they'll run out of charge before we even get one side of the ship thawed.
WAIT!
Here!
What are those?
Fancy lamps.
HOV-R1
ZIP
Huh?
ZIP

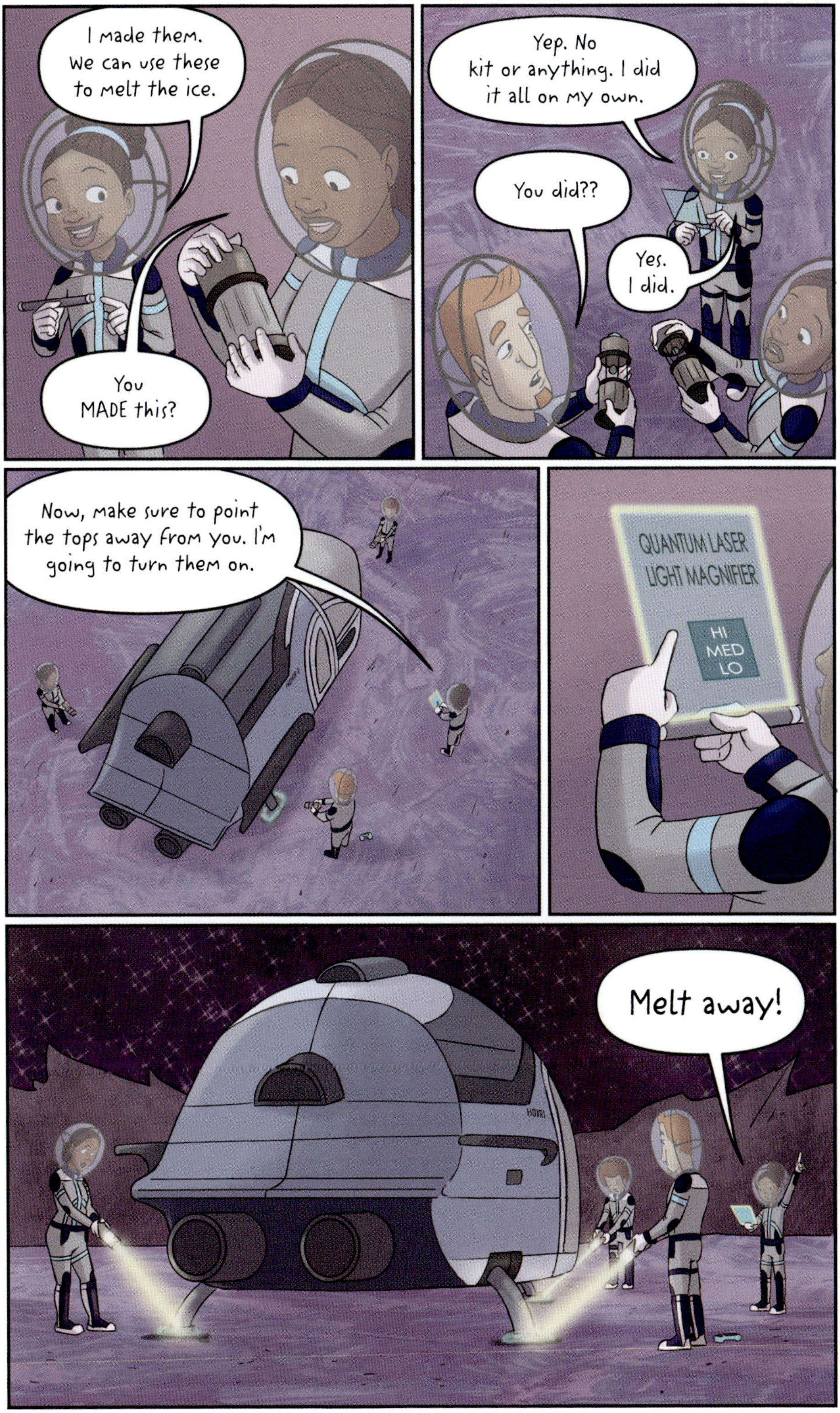
I made them. We can use these to melt the ice.
You MADE this?
Yep. No kit or anything. I did it all on my own.
You did??
Yes. I did.
Now, make sure to point the tops away from you. I'm going to turn them on.
QUANTUM LASER LIGHT MAGNIFIER
HI
MED
LO
Melt away!

Blake. Listen, honey.
I'm sorry I seemed so shocked, but I had no idea...
About what?
That you were capable of making something so...complex.
Oh. Well, it really was no big deal.
I'm just glad I could help. For once.
Blake—

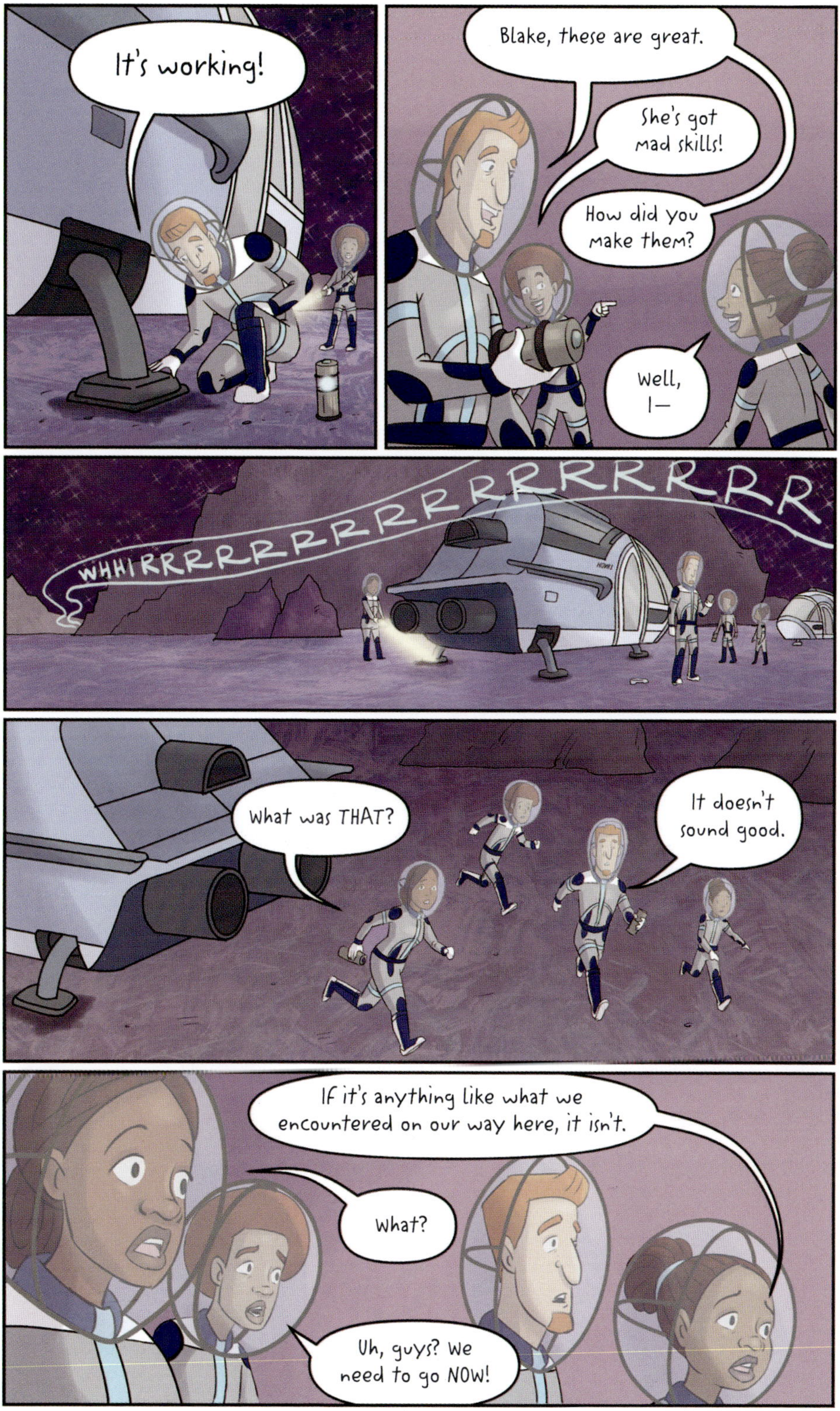

It's working!
Blake, these are great.
She's got mad skills!
How did you make them?
Well, I—
WHHIRRRRRRRRRRRRRRRRRRRRR
What was THAT?
It doesn't sound good.
If it's anything like what we encountered on our way here, it isn't.
What?
Uh, guys? We need to go NOW!

This way!
WWHIRRRRRR
RRRRRRR
HOVR1
I've never seen anything like those before.
That's because they're ALIEN ROBOTS!
Stay quiet.
They look meaner than the other ones we saw.

MEANER?
There's more?
Yeah, a bunch of little creepy-crawly ones.
And a cute one that blasted our hover. Because I touched it.
My blaster is in the hover. Alex?
Mine is sitting right next to yours, Frank.
Fantastic.
WHIRRRRRRR

WHIRRRRR
Blake! No!

What are you doing?
I'm increasing the range on the charger. If I can extend it to where the robots are standing—
then crank up the power— it should blow them to smithereens.
Um, any day now, Blake. They're getting closer.
I hope this works.

Which one?
Are you ready to fire it up?
I don't know. I can't do this. I'm no good.
You're right. You aren't good.

You are MUCH better than good. No one at this academy is just "good." And you are one of the brightest stars here.
But if that's true, my parents would be here.
I assure you, Blake, whether they're here or not says nothing about what a talented scientist you are.
If you say so.
I say so.

KERTHUNK!
KERTHUNK!
AAAAAAAAAHH
Blake, what's wrong? Crank up the charger!
I...I'm not sure if I can do it!

BLAKE!! BRODY!!
HELP!
Blake, hurry!
NOOOOOO!
MOM! DAD!

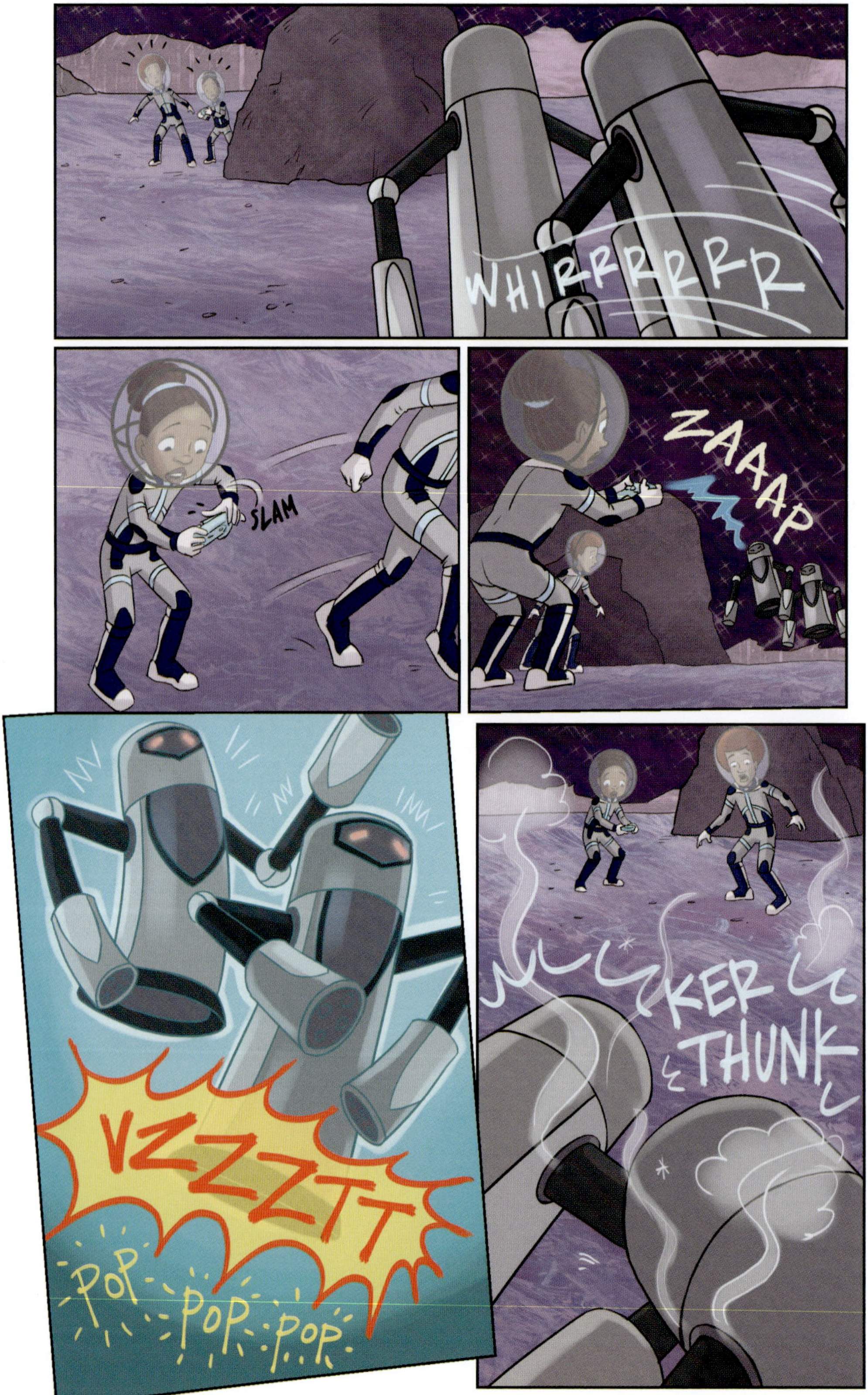
WHIRRRRRR
SLAM
ZAAAAP
VZZZTT
POP POP POP
KER THUNK

Woo-hoo! That was DYNAMITE! I hope I caught that on my body cam. I knew you could do it, Blake Laser.
Yeah—but not before the robots got to Mom and Dad.
Then we'll have to go with Plan B. Let's go find them. Come on!
Where are they?
How did they disappear so quickly?
Hang on. Let me go get my holo pad.

Let's go.
Do you have to touch everything?
Yes, I do. Check it out! There's something funny about these rocks, and by funny, I mean not normal.
TAP!
AHA!

What do you think it is?
It looks like some sort of security code panel.
In alien language! I bet the aliens rolled Mom and Dad back here. That's why they disappeared so fast.
And this could be a door.
Hang on a sec. I have a code cracker that I could try.
Hey—it's working!
WHIRRRRRR
Jackpot!
BEEEEP!

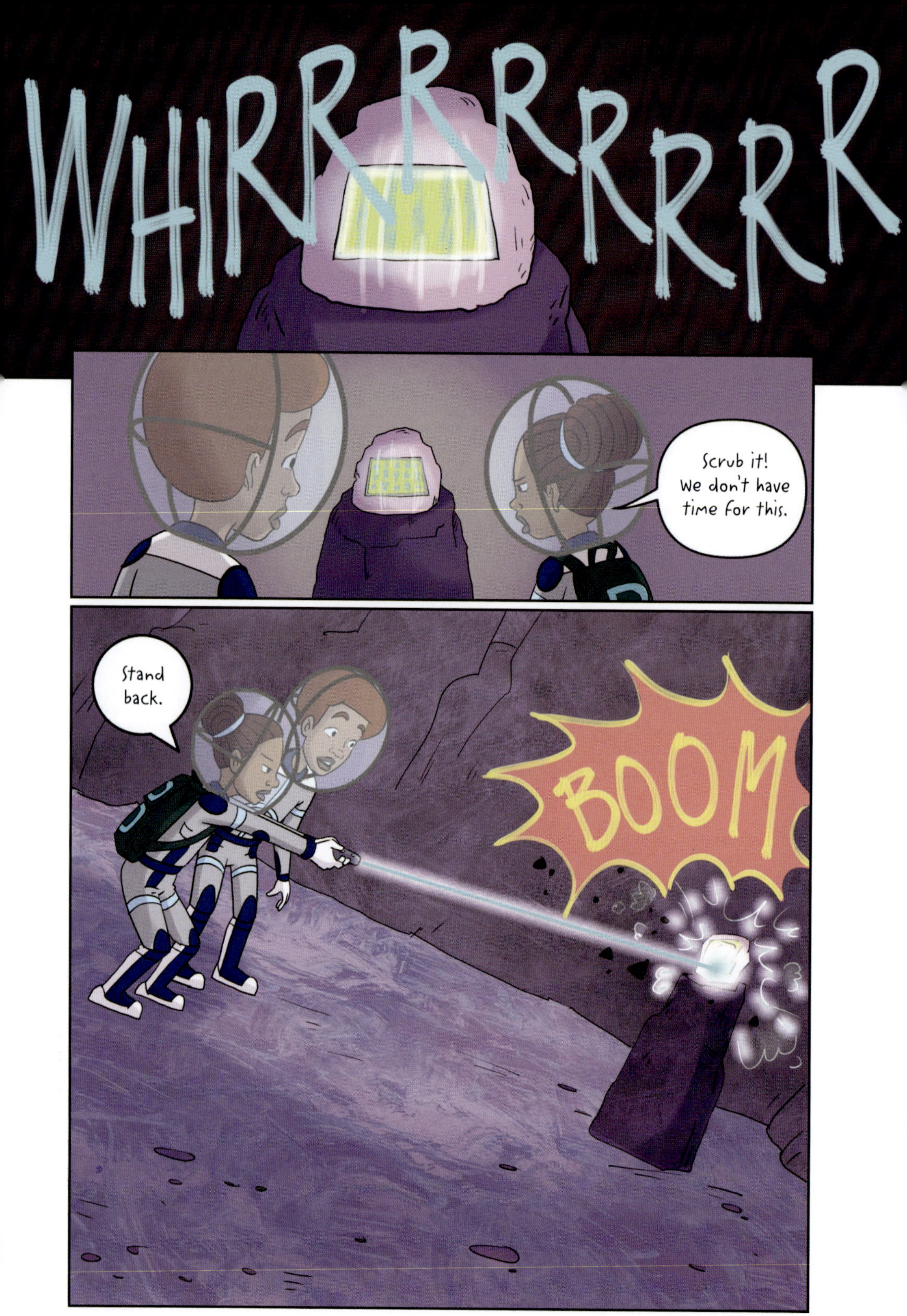
WHIRRRRRRRR
Scrub it! We don't have time for this.
Stand back.
BOOM

SHOOM
Sometimes you just have to do it old-school.
Can I try?
No!
Aww.

Chapter 7

Close Encounters of the Inane Kind

Something breached the main entry.
What do you mean "something"?
BEEP
BLIP!
Destroy it! Destroy it now!!
We don't even know what it is yet, Ultimate Supreme, sir.
SHOOM
POP!
POP!

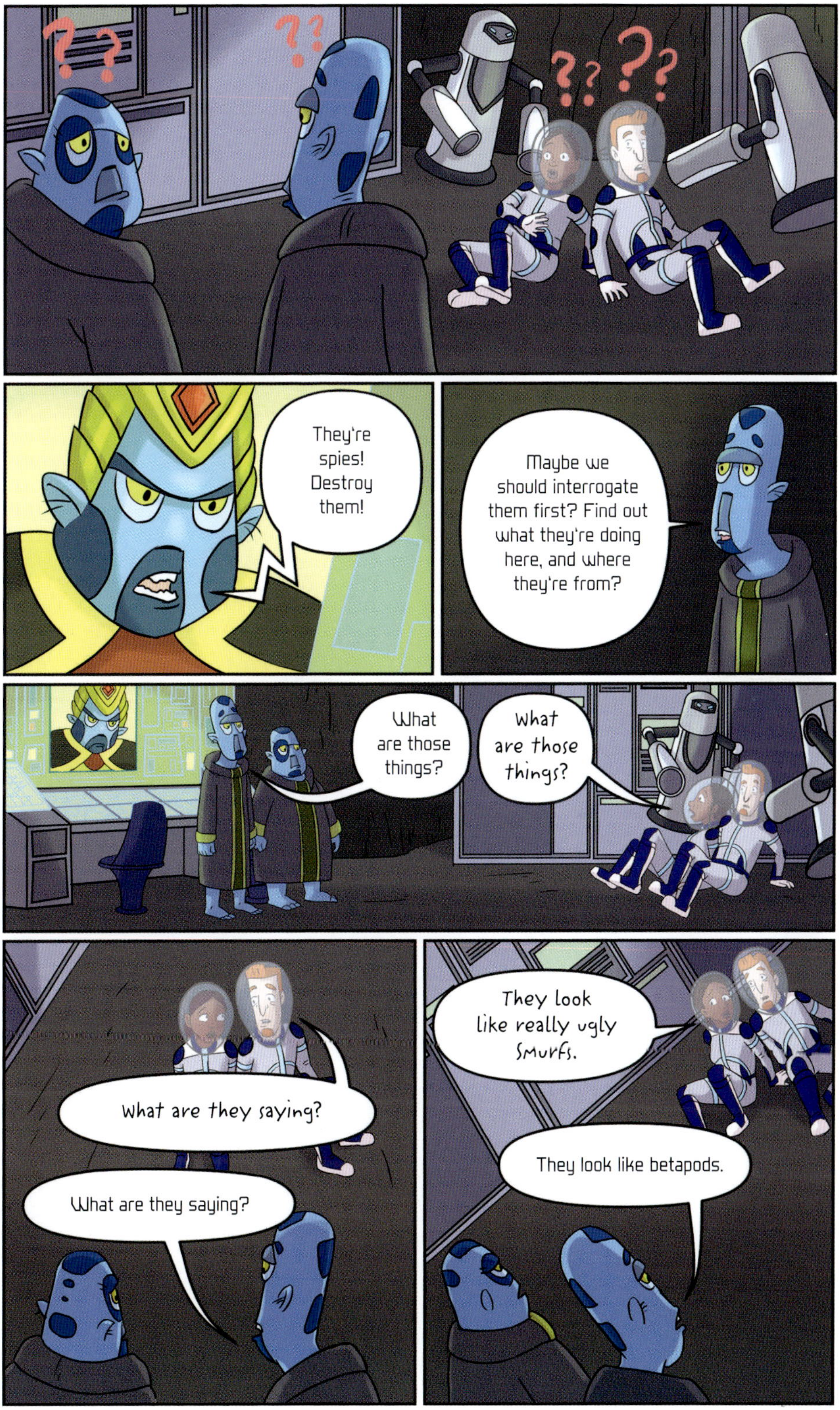

They're spies! Destroy them!
Maybe we should interrogate them first? Find out what they're doing here, and where they're from?
What are those things?
What are those things?
What are they saying?
What are they saying?
They look like really ugly Smurfs.
They look like betapods.

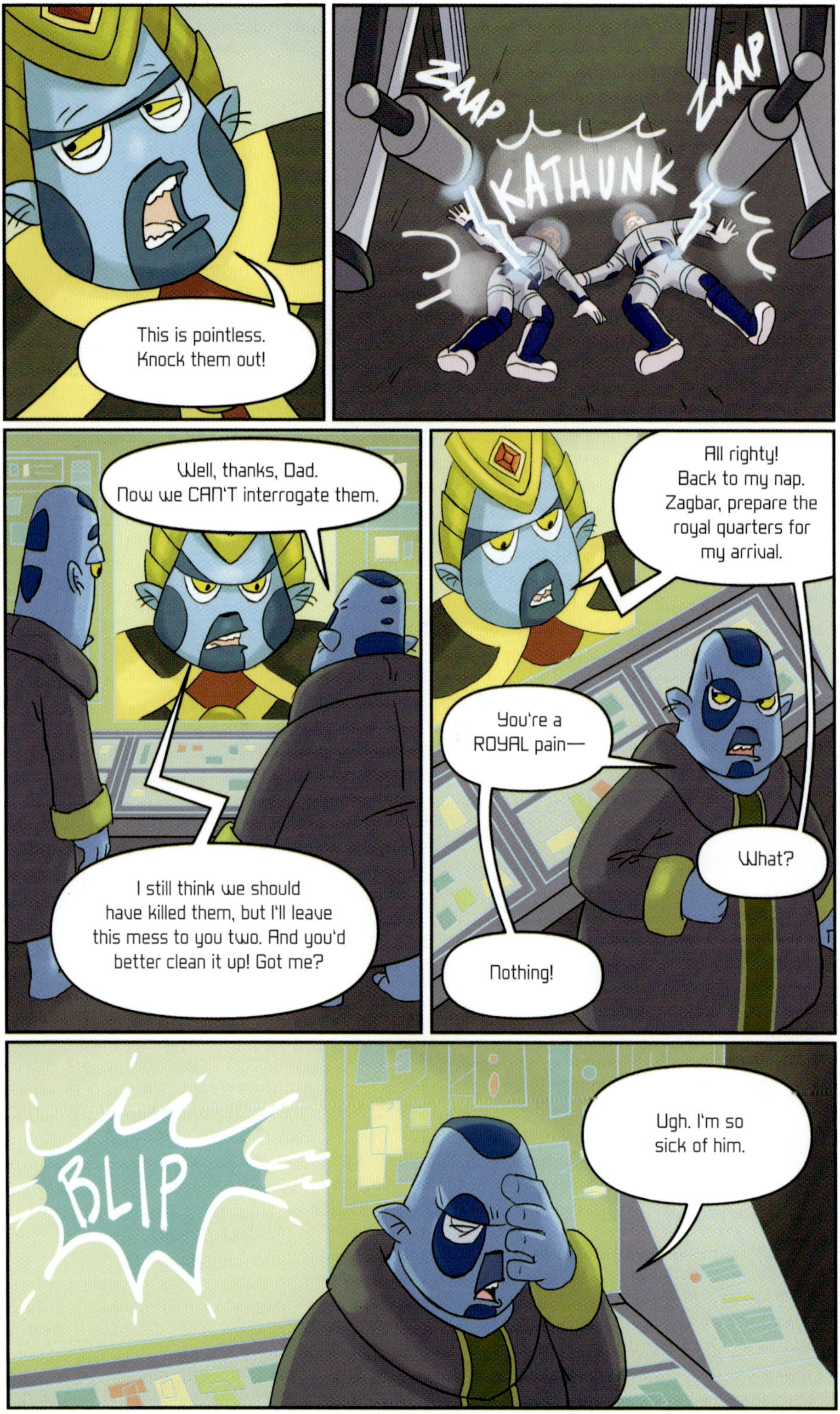
This is pointless. Knock them out!
ZAAP
ZAAP
KATHUNK
Well, thanks, Dad. Now we CAN'T interrogate them.
I still think we should have killed them, but I'll leave this mess to you two. And you'd better clean it up! Got me?
All righty! Back to my nap. Zagbar, prepare the royal quarters for my arrival.
You're a ROYAL pain—
What?
Nothing!
BLIP
Ugh. I'm so sick of him.

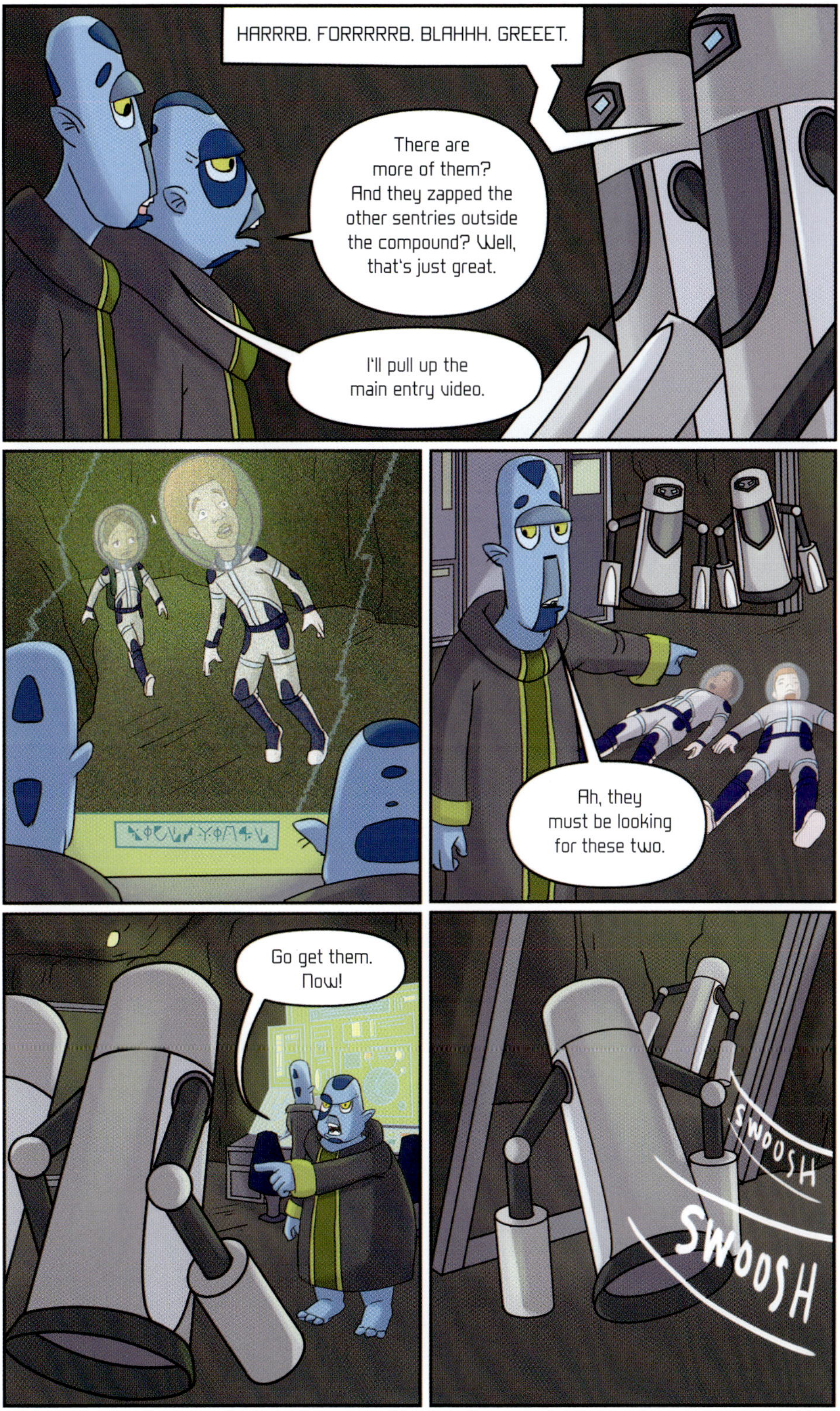
HARRRB. FORRRRRB. BLAHHH. GREEET.
There are more of them? And they zapped the other sentries outside the compound? Well, that's just great.
I'll pull up the main entry video.
Ah, they must be looking for these two.
Go get them. Now!
SWOOSH
SWOOSH

How's it looking, Blake?
Let's see...
I've scanned the compound. There are life-forms right here. This could be them!
Let's check it out.

ZAAP
Where did you learn to shoot like that?
CLANK!
Uh, at the academy. Yeah. It was an elective.
I'm not sure I believe you.

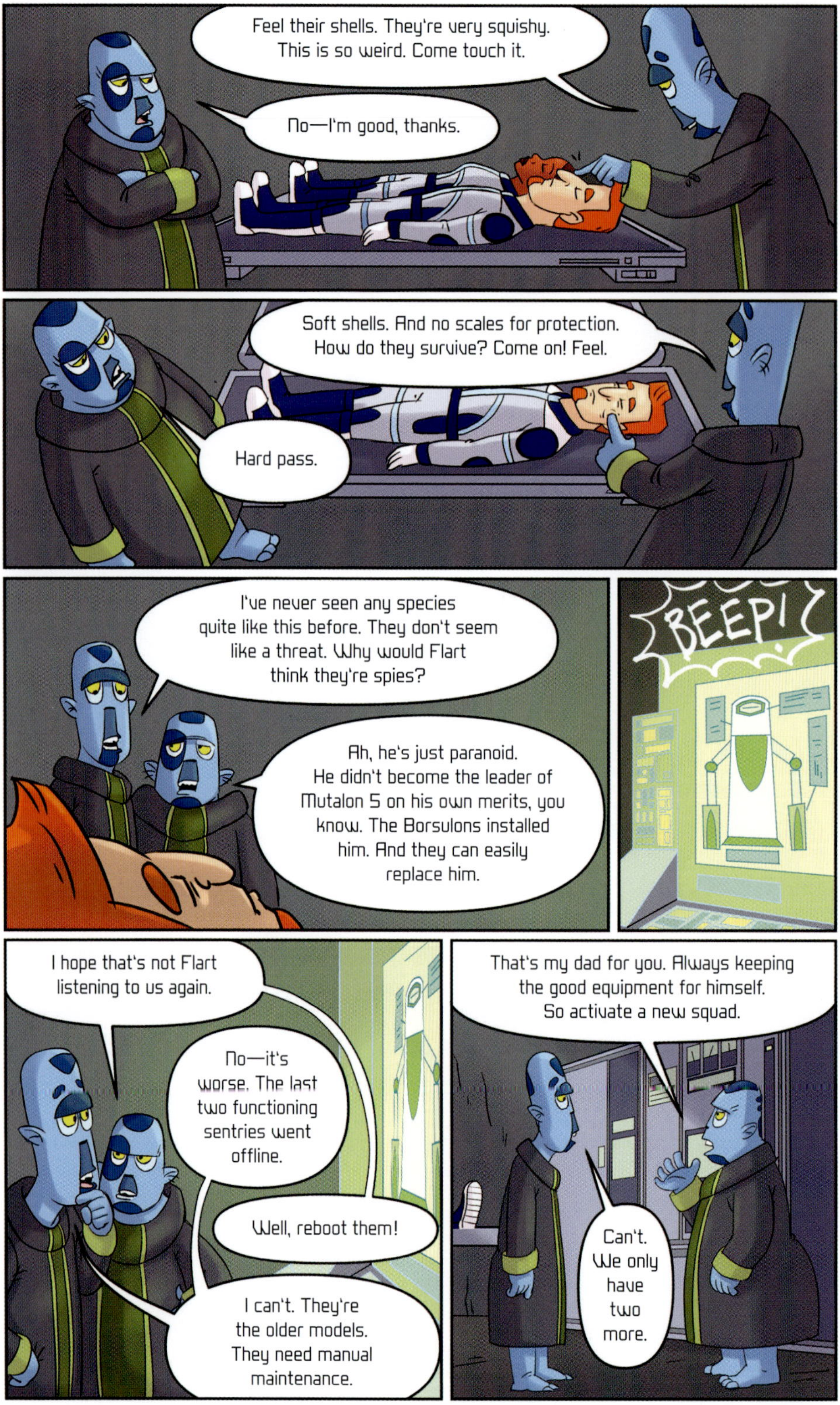
Feel their shells. They're very squishy. This is so weird. Come touch it.
No—I'm good, thanks.
Soft shells. And no scales for protection. How do they survive? Come on! Feel.
Hard pass.
I've never seen any species quite like this before. They don't seem like a threat. Why would Flart think they're spies?
Ah, he's just paranoid. He didn't become the leader of Mutalon 5 on his own merits, you know. The Borsulons installed him. And they can easily replace him.
BEEP!
I hope that's not Flart listening to us again.
No—it's worse. The last two functioning sentries went offline.
Well, reboot them!
I can't. They're the older models. They need manual maintenance.
That's my dad for you. Always keeping the good equipment for himself. So activate a new squad.
Can't. We only have two more.

SNOR-GIT! Just activate the last two then.
They're still being calibrated for the local environment. We'll be notified when they're online.
Of course we will.
What should we do in the meantime? The other creatures are coming this way.
Hmm... Do we have the new control units?
Yes, but they haven't been tested. There could be some glitches.
That's okay. Let's get these two things to the maintenance cell and fire up the new program. They'll make good bait!

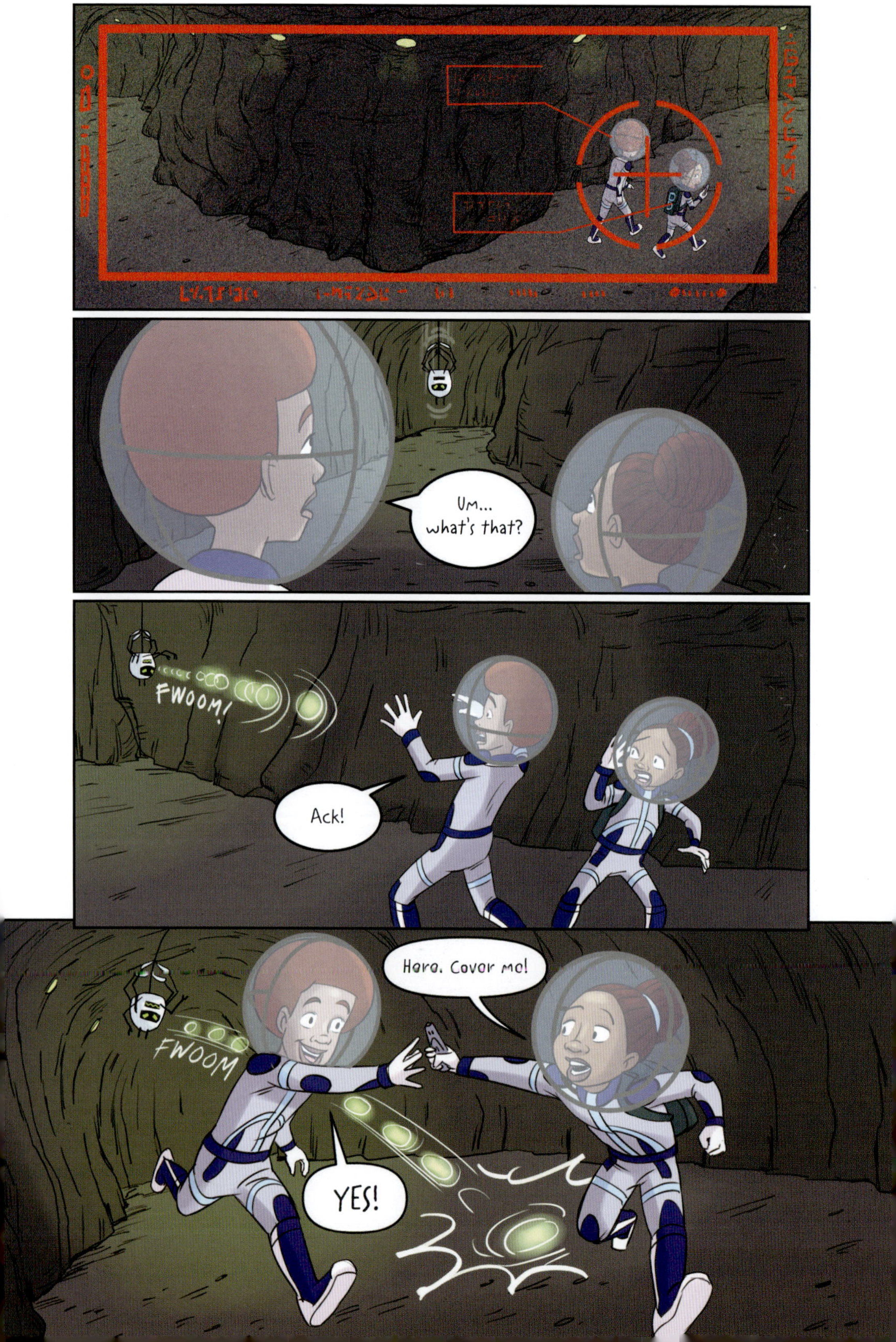
Um... what's that?
FWOOM!
Ack!
Here. Cover me!
FWOOM
YES!

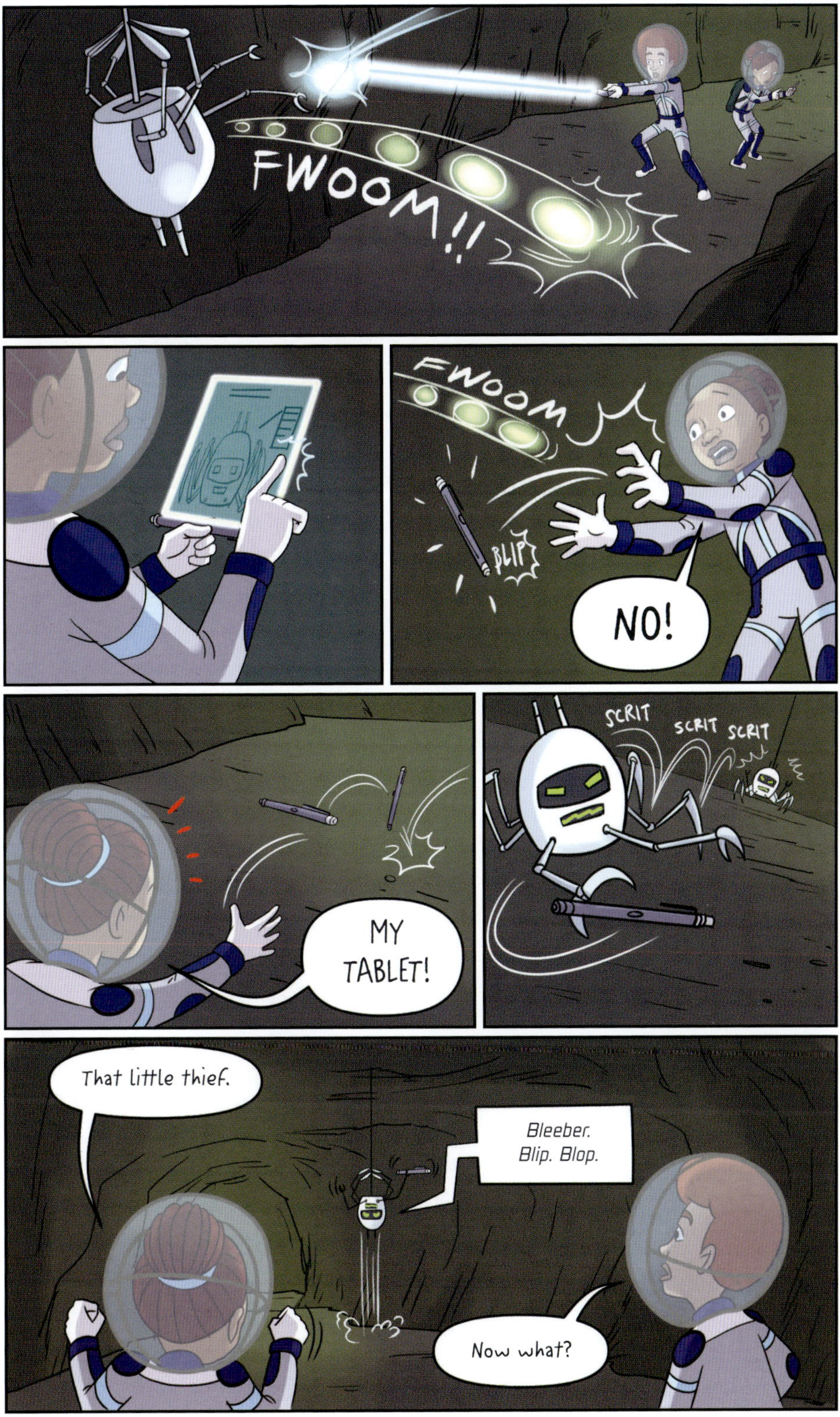
FWOOM!!
FWOOM
BLIP
NO!
MY TABLET!
SCRIT
SCRIT
SCRIT
That little thief.
Bleeber. Blip. Blop.
Now what?

Hm...
Ooh! Maybe I can connect to my holo pad.
BEEP BEEP
I'm in.
Whoa!
PAUSE
SCRIT SCRIT
BLIP

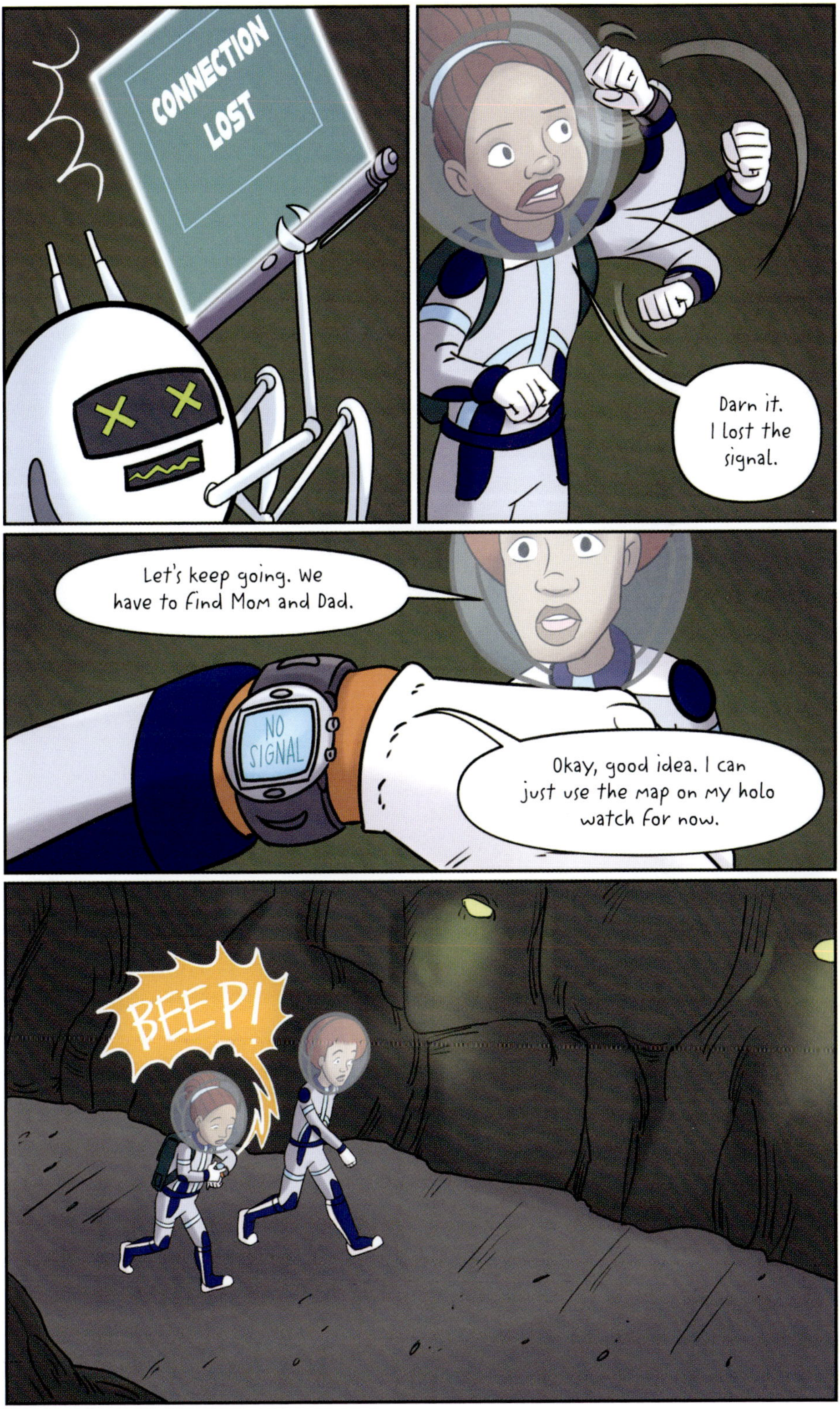
CONNECTION LOST
Darn it. I lost the signal.
Let's keep going. We have to find Mom and Dad.
NO SIGNAL
Okay, good idea. I can just use the map on my holo watch for now.
BEEP!

BEEP!!
What was that?
I have no clue. None of our tech sounds like that!
It must be the intruders. We need to get out of here!
What do we do with these things?
Just leave them here. Come on!

The life-forms have split up. We're close to two of them. Get your blaster ready.

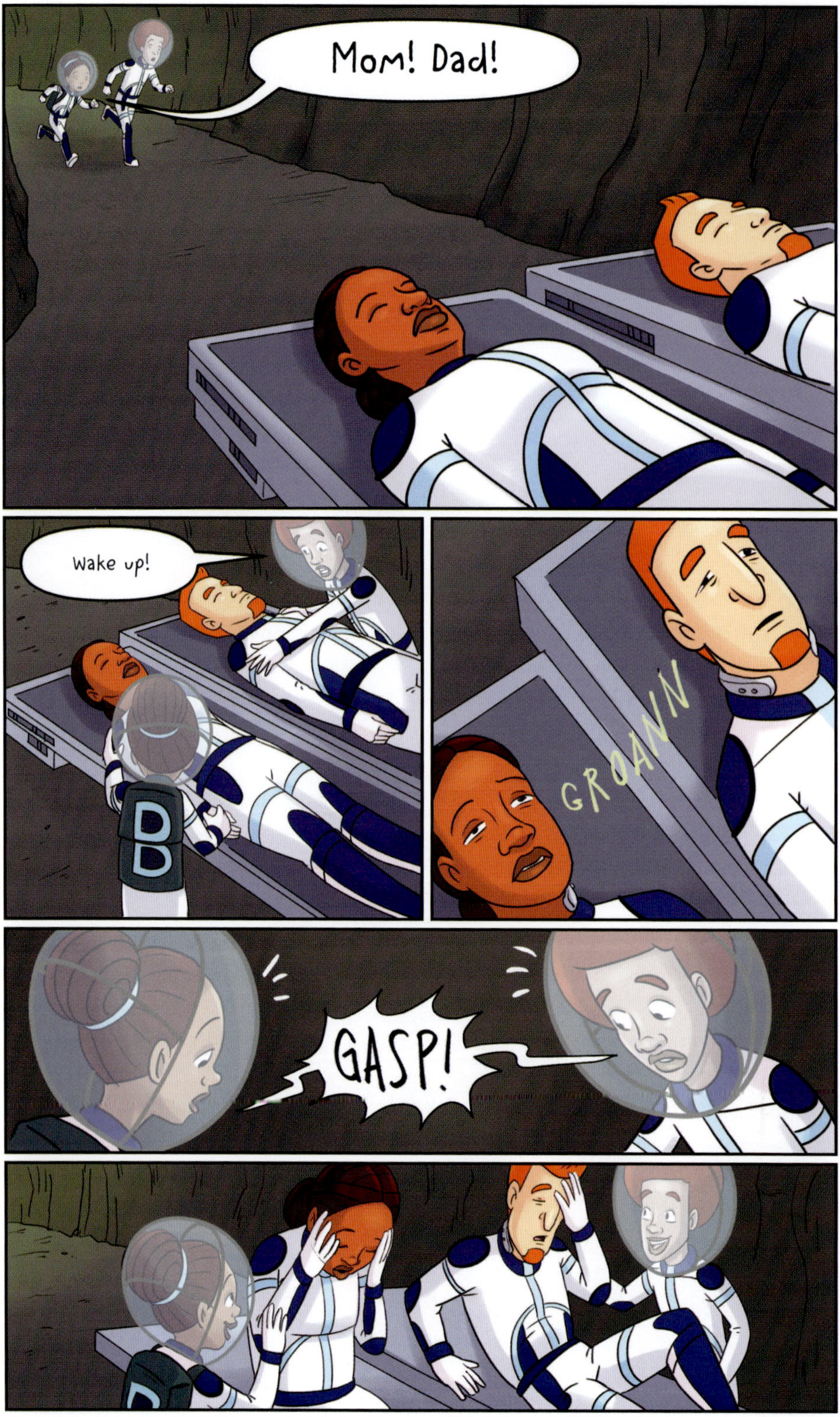
Mom! Dad!
Wake up!
GROANN
GASP!

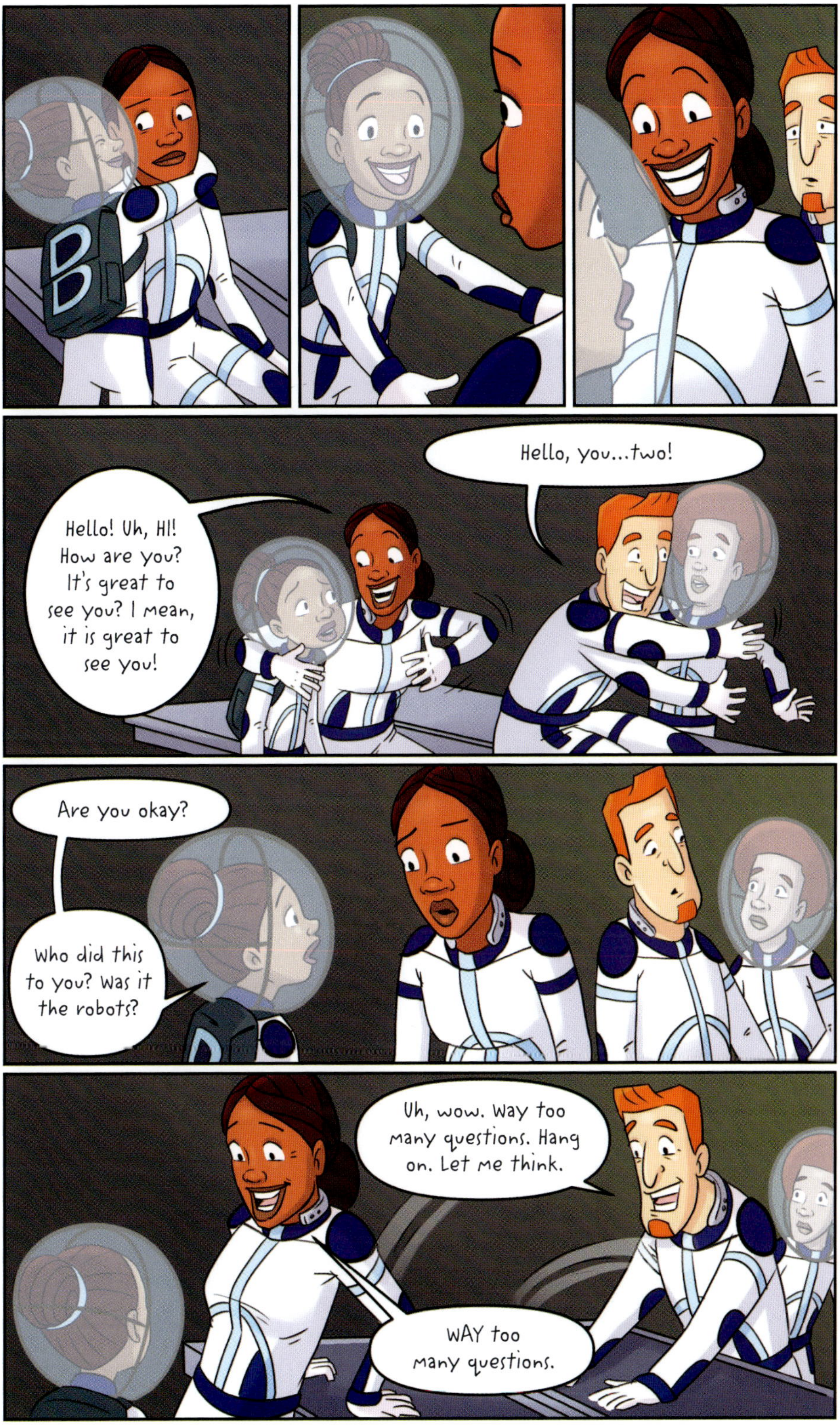
Hello, you...two!
Hello! Uh, HI! How are you? It's great to see you? I mean, it is great to see you!
Are you okay?
Who did this to you? Was it the robots?
Uh, wow. Way too many questions. Hang on. Let me think.
WAY too many questions.

Let's go.
Don't we need to get to the source of the signal?
WHAT? Is that why you're here?
SMACK
I mean, oh! Sure! It's that way.
Yeah, that way.
What is UP with them?
I don't know, but I'm not getting a stable enough reading on the oxygen levels in here yet.
Their shields really shouldn't be down.
B
Hey, uh, Mom, Dad? Why are your shields down?
Uh, we don't need them.
Yeah, Zagbar and Karl said we were fine without them. They are totally cool guys. The best!
SMACK
OOOF
Hey! They wouldn't say that! They don't know our names. We haven't been formally introduced.

Karl and Zagbar? Weren't those the names we heard on the hover?
SHOOM
SHOOM
Yes. Something strange is going on. Get in front of Mom and Dad—and see if you can tell where they are headed.
I'll scout ahead.
Are you done, nerd?
Yes. That was fun. Thank you. What's a nerd?

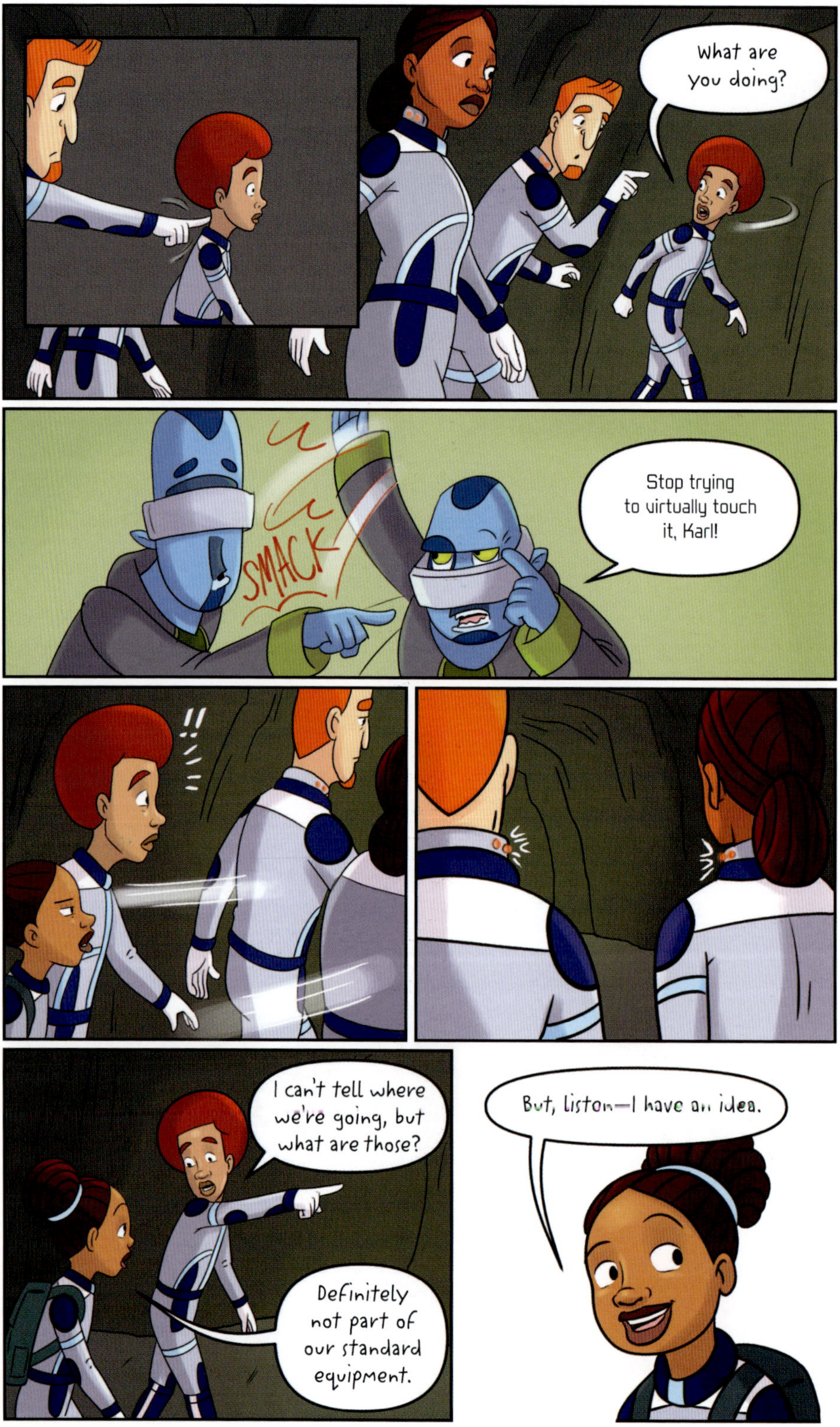
What are you doing?
Stop trying to virtually touch it, Karl!
SMACK
!!
I can't tell where we're going, but what are those?
Definitely not part of our standard equipment.
But, listen—I have an idea.

It's up that way.
They're almost to the cell. We just need to get them all in there and seal it.
FREEZE

WHACK!
What happened?? They stopped responding.
I don't know. The system froze. They're stuck!
See?? It glitched! What do we do now?
I know.
We'll have to sneak up on them from behind and push them into the cell. Let's go!
SHOOM
KLUNK

Now!
WHOOSH
Aliens—
DON'T
MOVE!
I don't know why
I just said that. They probably
can't understand me.
I've never
seen that shade
of blue before.

Get in there!
Uh, Blake? They're freaking me out a little.
ZZZAAAP
Aaaahhhhhh!

SMACK
ZHOOM
Nice work, Brody!
Let's turn our helpful friends off.
HOLOGRAM OFF
BLIP

TCHK
TCHK
Blake? Brody?
What happened?
I think you were under some sort of mind control.
How did you get away from those robots at the hover?
I disabled them with the modified hov-bat charger. Then after we broke into the cave and disabled a couple more with one of my laser blas—uh, shooting device things—
I used my mapping module to locate you and fooled those two whatever they are with my holo projector.
It's a blaster.

Yeah. We met them already. Let me see that.
You've got quite the arsenal here, Blake.
You made these too?
Yeah. They're just more of my "toys," Mom.
And we wouldn't even let her charge the hover.
It looks like she could have handled it just fine.
But I was the one who found the ice poo!
Yes, you did, Brody. Nice work.
Now let's see if you can locate the source of the signal we've been sent here to find. Come on!

Chapter 8

The Same Boat

B

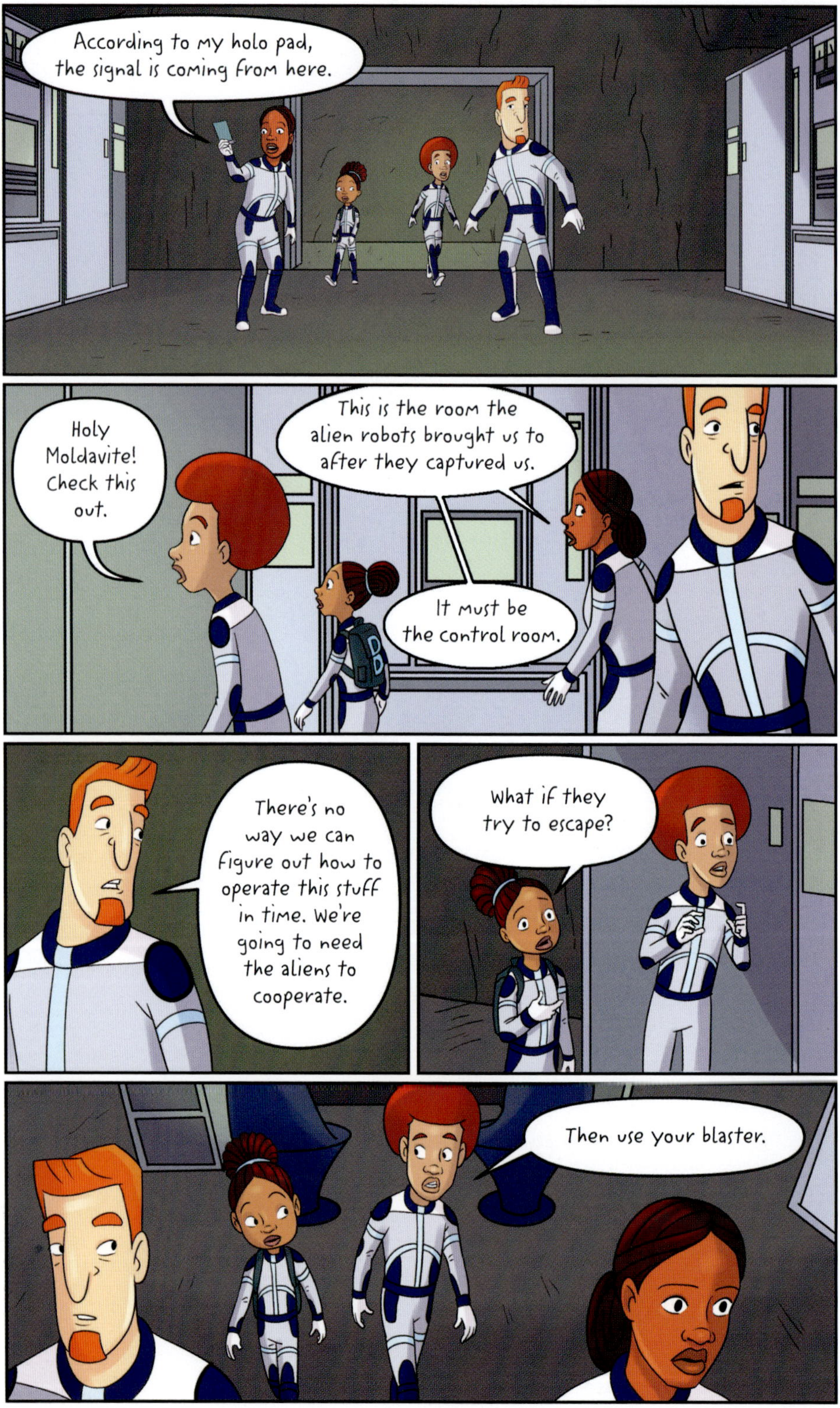
According to my holo pad, the signal is coming from here.
Holy Moldavite! Check this out.
This is the room the alien robots brought us to after they captured us.
It must be the control room.
There's no way we can figure out how to operate this stuff in time. We're going to need the aliens to cooperate.
What if they try to escape?
Then use your blaster.

SMACK
ZHOOM
You're coming with us. Our planet is in danger, and you're going to help us fix it.
Ha ada oka.
Adi mama ani.
Kedo ita zorf neeta kepi. He netu anyo aka bang.
What are they saying?

TRANSLATE
PLAYBACK
They pushed us! Yeah, they're mean! And they're pointing weapons at us too. I want to go home.
BEEP
Of course you have an alien translator on your holo watch.
With a frequency decoder for real-time translation!
Let me put the program on your watch too. I can set it to translate both languages so they'll also be able to understand us.
Can you understand what I'm saying?
Yes!

I am Frank McClain and this is my family, Alex, Brody, and Blake.
My name is Karl, and this is my associate—
Boss!
SMACK!
Fine. My BOSS, Zagbar. We are from the planet Mutalon 5 in the Algorian star system.
So YOU'RE Karl and Zagbar. Hey! I have a friend named Karl!
It's short for Karlobleepen.
Oh, that's cool. My friend is just Karl.
Brody! Stop fraternizing with the creatures. We're trying to interrogate them!
We're from the planet Earth, which is in grave danger. We received information that our sun's energy is being siphoned from a source on Asteroid FBX7.
And the signal we followed led us right to your base.
Yes, that's correct. We're using your star to charge our own. It needs constant fueling to keep our planet alive. And even the energy from your star won't be enough for us.

How are you getting the energy to your star?
By using the Borsulon Star Charger 8000 v2. V1 had a few "issues."
Come to think of it, I really miss our friends in the Nomouri star system.
Anyway, the Borsulon Star Charger 8000 v2 system generates an uber-dense gravitational field, which draws energy from your star and directs it to the closest wormhole.
It travels through space and comes out another wormhole near our star system. The beam is then injected into the core of our star.
Fascinating. But why our star? Why don't you just use one that is closer?
We just go where we're told.
I think it has something to do with finding a wormhole that best suits the energy transfer, which aren't that easy to locate.
So you're going to kill our planet to save yours?
If you need a new planet, go find another one. Not our problem.
YOU'RE gonna have a problem if you don't turn your energy-sucking extracting thing off!

Looks like Dad has been brushing up on his tough-guy talk.
It's not up to us! We're not in charge. We're just here to monitor the system. Flart is in charge!
What's a Flart?
The Ultimate Supreme Flart.
He's the leader of our planet. He used to be just Supreme Flart, but he was promoted to Ultimate Supreme.
It was a self-promotion.
Where is this "Flart"?
He's en route from our home planet. But you're wasting your time. Even if he wanted to help, he'd have to get approval from the Borsulons.
The Borsulons? What are they? Are they blue too?
Pink, actually. The Borsulons supply us with all our technological needs in exchange for the crystals and metals we mine for them on our planet.
It's a win-win.

Listen, if you don't get ahold of this Flart or the Borsulons or SOMEONE, it's gonna be a LOSE-LOSE for you two!
Well done, Dad. Well done.
Perhaps a different approach, Frank.
Planet Earth and its moon are home to billions of human beings. If our sun dies, then we'll all die too.
Please call your superiors for us. There's got to be another way.
There's nothing we can do.
I'm sorry. There isn't.
Isn't there anything you can do at all? If you're able to receive video signals from Earth, then you could see what you're destroying.
I am actually curious what their planet is like. Zagbar, don't you want to look?
Fine, but it won't make a difference.

Ugh. The console short-circuited again.
Great. Do we have another one of those?
Yeah. Give me a sec.
WHOA! WHOA! EASY THERE, PARTNER!
No need to be alarmed. These only work on inanimate objects.

BEEP!
It's called the Size Shifter XL.
ZAAP
SHRINK
WHOOSH!
ZAAP!

Whoa.
That...is really cool!
The Size Shifter XL is yet another Borsulon product that could only be built with the crystals found in our star system.
It's very handy for shrinking and enlarging inanimate objects—especially all the equipment we needed to bring here.
BEEP!
What if you shoot a shrink ray at the ray of another shrink ray that is being shot?
Does only the shrink ray's ray shrink, or does the shrink ray ITSELF shrink too?
My mind is so blown right now.

Okay, here we go. Videos of planet Earth.
BLIP
BREAKING NEWS
IS EARTH DOOMED?
BREAKING NEWS
IS EARTH DOOMED?
HAWAII SEES SNOW FOR THE FIRST TIME IN FOREVER
RECORD BITTER BLAST
COLD
COLD
COLD
COLD
I can't believe it. Everything looks so cold and dark. People must be freezing. My poor friends!
Maybe we can figure out how to turn off their energy extracting system and save our planet!

I would strongly advise against that. If you try to tamper with the system, the Borsulons will be alerted, which will disrupt their business.
They wouldn't hesitate to wipe out you and your planet as a result.
That may be true, but we have nothing to lose.
I hate to do this, but we're running out of time. So I'm only going to ask you once. How do we access your energy-extracting system? Show us right now!
Okay, but the controls to turn off the system are...in a different part of the compound!
Well, let's go, then. Move!

Chapter 9

THE LONGEST SHOT

You're making a BIG mistake.
Just keep moving!
Yep, he's still got it.
FUMBLE
FUMBLE
Well, maybe not ALL of it.

It's just up ahead.
What are you doing?!
I need to open the door.
Go ahead.
WHOOSH

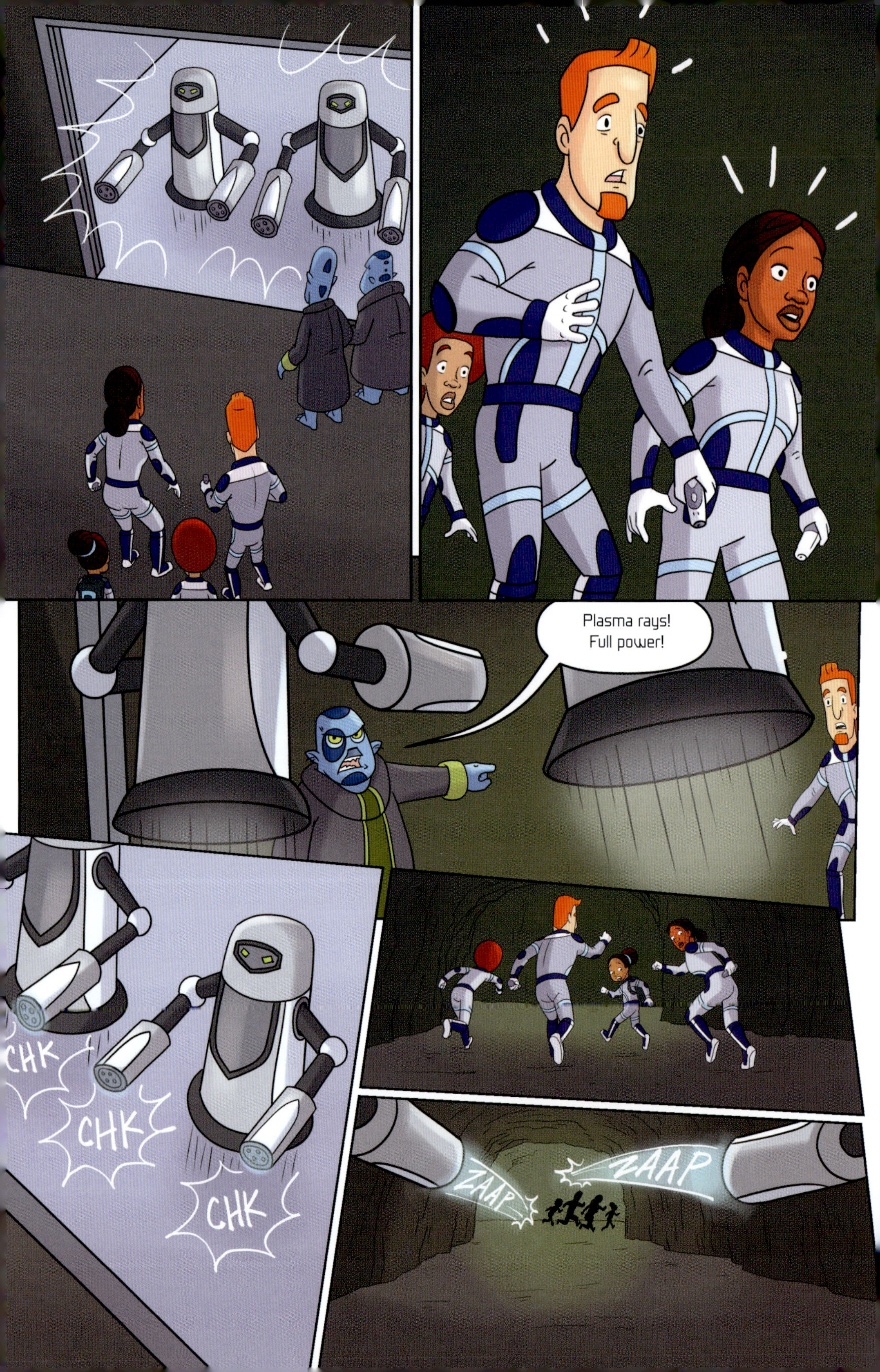
Plasma rays!
Full power!
CHK
CHK
CHK
ZAAP
ZAAP

ZAAP
ZAAP
ZAAP
ZAAP
ZAAP
Quick! It looks like a way out.
ZAAP
ZAAP
ZAAP
ZAAP
ZAAP

THUNK
THUNK
There's no way out.
Hey!!
NO!
ZAAP
I knew I shouldn't have trusted you. Let us out of here, you slippery skink.
I don't think so.

What do we do?
I don't know. This cell looks like solid rock, but maybe we can figure out how to disarm the shield.
Good idea. I'll take a look.
Blake, can you use your watch to get us out of here?
There's only so much it can do, Brody. I mean, it's a piece of tech, not a sledge-hammer.
Yeah, but you've made such cool stuff. Like when you blew up those robot aliens with the hov-bat charger!
That was pretty awesome, huh?
I think I caught that on my body cam. Wanna watch a replay?
Sure, why not?

PLAY
ZAAP!
Yeah!
BOOM

Any luck, Dad?
I'm afraid not. And I...I don't know if we have any other options.
What are you watching?
Just some videos from our family vacation.
ZAAP
Look how awesome she is!

You both are.
And we're sorry we missed a lot of it.
We have it all on the body cam footage.
No, I'm not talking about just on this trip. I'm talking about everything.
Your mom is right. We missed out on a lot. I wish we could go back in time and do it again.
You are both so talented, but we clearly didn't realize to what extent. Your father and I didn't take the time to notice the things we should have. You both deserved more of our attention.
Brody, I should have shown more appreciation for your creativity.
That's okay, Dad.
And, Blake, I never imagined you could make all those things!
You mean my LITTLE inventions?
Blake. Sometimes LITTLE inventions can be a lot BIGGER than you think.
Thanks, Dad.

Oh, kids. Come here—
Bring it in.
That was nice. Now what do we do?
"Bigger than you think"...
Dad? Mom? I think I can do it.
Do what?
Save the world?

How?
With one of these.
You can save the world with a FANCY LAMP?
Maybe. But we have to get ahold of Karl and Zagbar. Let me see if I can get their attention.
OPEN ALL FREQUENCIES
They're not going to just let us out. They don't trust us—especially Zagbar.
HMM...
He may not trust us, but we know who he DOES trust. Or fear, at least.

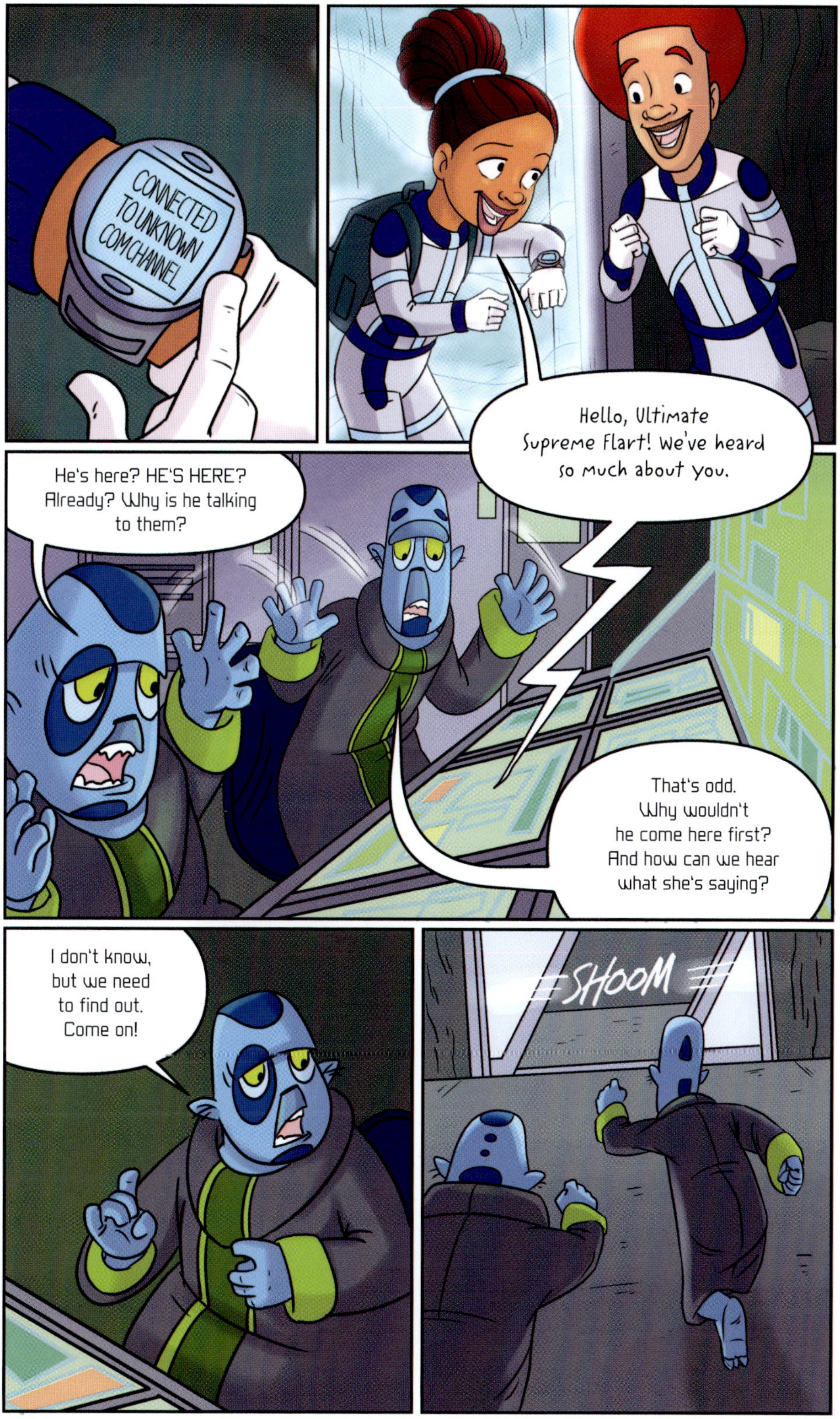
CONNECTED TO UNKNOWN COM CHANNEL
Hello, Ultimate Supreme Flart! We've heard so much about you.
He's here? HE'S HERE? Already? Why is he talking to them?
That's odd. Why wouldn't he come here first? And how can we hear what she's saying?
I don't know, but we need to find out. Come on!
SHOOM

Where is he? Where's Flart? Did he leave already?
PANT PANT
You tricked us, didn't you?
Yes, I'm sorry. But I think I figured out a way to provide all the energy that Mutalon 5 could ever use, and I need your help.
We're listening—
KARL is listening.
If you take us back to the control room, we'll be happy to show you!
Nope. No way.
But what if they really can do what they're saying?
Why should we trust them? They've already tricked us once.
It could be a much better solution than what we're dealing with now. We'll be careful.

Fine, you can come—but only two of you, in case you try any more funny business.
Great! Well, I have to go...and I need Brody to come with me.
Well, okay, then. You can do it, guys!
Good luck!

I have a device that just may be able to generate all the energy your star needs without killing our sun.
You'll never have to worry again. Well, at least for a couple million years.
How?
First, I need to know if your Size Shifter XL can make objects bigger than their original size.
I don't know. We've never tried to make objects even bigger, since that wouldn't make sense for space travel.
Can I take a look at one? Please?
Zagbar?
Fine.

Thanks!

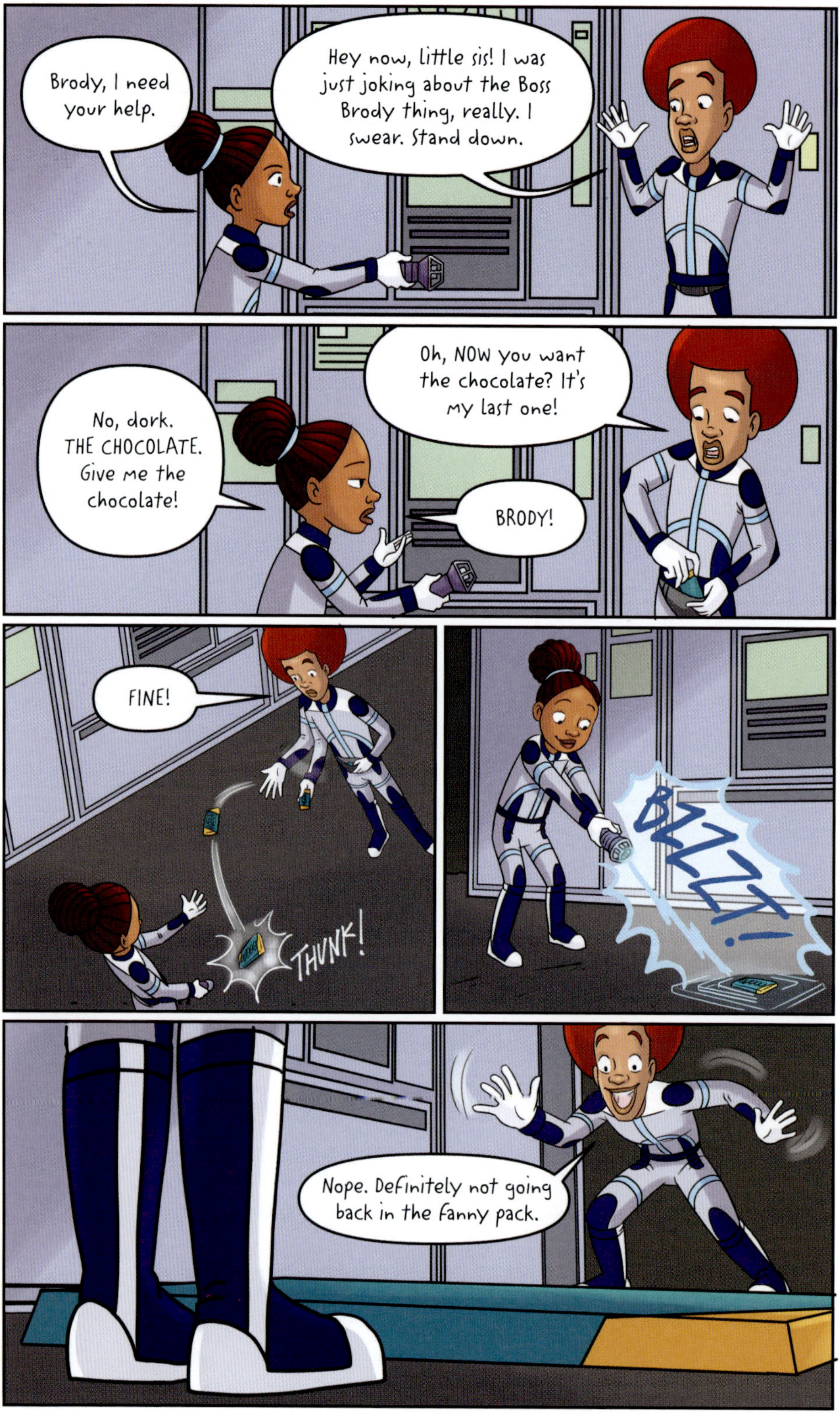
Brody, I need your help.
Hey now, little sis! I was just joking about the Boss Brody thing, really. I swear. Stand down.
No, dork. THE CHOCOLATE. Give me the chocolate!
Oh, NOW you want the chocolate? It's my last one!
BRODY!
FINE!
THUNK!
BZZZT!
Nope. Definitely not going back in the fanny pack.

Karl, can your rocket ships be piloted via remote control?
They have to be. We have no clue how to pilot those things. We just input the coordinates and it takes us to our destination.
Great. Could we use them?
Maybe. Zagbar?
No! Definitely not. This is getting way out of control.
Come on, Zagbar. Let's at least hear their plan first.
Who are YOU to tell ME what to do?!
BEEP
Please. I think I can really help your planet.
If anybody can do it, Blake Laser can. She's a genius.
Aw—thanks, Brody.

Zagbar, they just want their planet to survive. And they're helping us too. What if we no longer had to worry about our star dying? We wouldn't have to depend on the Borsulons any longer.
No. Take them back to the cell.
Zagbar, listen to me. All you do is complain about doing whatever your dad tells you to do and believe me...
I KNOW what it's like being told what to do ALL THE TIME. Wouldn't you rather do your own thinking than always having your dad do it for you?
You'd better watch your tone, Karl.
Look, If you give them a chance, maybe you won't have to jump through every hoop in the universe for...
FLART anymore!

Karl? Did you just call him—
That's right! I just called him FLART!
Wow, Karl—you're willing to risk mind control for this?
Yes, Zagbar. I am. I'm sick of living like this. Aren't you?
Proceed.
All right!
Brody, I need your mad skills now. Just draw what I'm saying, okay?
Easy-peasy, black hole squeezy.
ENABLE AIR CANVAS

My quantum laser light amplifier—aka fancy lamp—takes an energy source and magnifies it exponentially.
Now, imagine if it were 1,000 times bigger. Think how much energy that would create.
What we need to do is launch one out to an optimal orbit around the sun, which will be used as the energy source.
We will send it with the modified Size Shifter XL. Both the q.l.l.m. and the size shifter will be controlled remotely with modules that I can create.
We fire the size shifter at the fancy lamp, and it gets HUGE!
Awesome! BY BRODY
You turn on your system at a tiny fraction of what it's at now, I engage the q.l.l.m. and voilà! Energy for your planet that should last a million years.

Nice work, Brody.
How does that sound, Zagbar?
Promising, but it doesn't matter what I think. My dad won't go for it.
So don't tell him.
It doesn't matter. Krutahna will still find out. And when she does, we're all in deep doogon.
If Krutahna *doesn't* find a new star for us, we're doomed anyway. I think we should take the chance.
So how 'bout it, Zagnut? What do you think?
NUDGE NUDGE
Well, I *am* tired of dealing with all my dad's drama.
NUDGE NUDGE

You really think you can do this?
Yes, absolutely.
Well, you know what I think? I think I'm done letting my dad think for me. Let's do it! But we have to hurry. My dad really will be here soon.
Okay, first things first. I need to hack into the control module and reprogram it so that we'll have fully functioning operational abilities. Karl, can you help me with that while Brody gets my magnifier units in the hover? And, Zagbar, can you free my parents?
On it!
Sure thing. And we'll all meet at the launching bay.
Of course.

BEEP
Brody, this way!
BEEP

Chapter 10
Charitable Betrayal

DROP YOUR WEAPONS!
FWOOM
FWOOM
FWOOM
FWOOM
FWOOM
FWOOM
Not again.
Dad! Seriously?! I'm your son!
Ah, my REBELLIOUS son, indeed.
Rebellious? What are you talking about?
I overheard EVERY word about the treasonous little shindig you were planning.
Karl, I thought you turned off the communication system?
I thought I did too.
Ha! You did. It *was* off, but then you turned it back on!
Karl!
You must have activated the signal when you *leaned* up against the console...with your butt.
You mean when you PUSHED me *onto* the console??
Karl? Did you butt-dial me? Ha! I'm usually the one who does the butt-dialing around here.
Look at this thing. There's a LOT of butt-dialing happening with it.

I'm sorry, Zagbar.
Enough with the chitter.
Wait one moment.
Not too much now. We don't want you splitting in two!
SPLOOT!
SLURP SLURP
That's so cute! What is it?

Why thank you. I'm a Mutaloneon.
It's a zorf. Obviously.
Not you, that!
Right. So, where were we?
Oh yeah.
The treasoning. You're conspiring against me, eh?
We're just trying to save your planet!
What IS that?
I am a human. My name is Blake Laser!
Blake what-now?
Did she say her name was Blake LASER?
BLAKE LASER!
Quiet! And where are you from, Blake Laser?
We're from planet Earth, which you're about to kill by draining all the energy from our sun. I can show you pictures, if you'd like.
SWIPE

That's Earth.
Humph. It's got potential. A bit too green though.
There's intelligent life on this one!
And who are YOU to say they are INTELLIGENT, hmm?
Blake has figured out a way to save our star without ever having to worry about finding another fuel source.
Who cares? We have the Borsulons for that.
Well, maybe not, sir.
Karl? What do you mean?
Krutahna said—
You spoke with Krutahna?!
Yes, sir. Madam Krutahna said that she may not have a new star before this one fizzles. Blake can help—
Oh, no, no. I cannot have a tiny soft-shelled bug help ME. The Borsulons would think I'm weak. Besides, Krutahna always comes through.
But this tiny soft-shelled bug may have a permanent solution, not just a temporary fix.

Karl. That's enough! Either you two behave or it's mind-control prison time!
Oh, please. You wouldn't do that to your own son.
Try me.
That's what I thought. We need to dispose of these annoying bugs immediately.
"Bug"?
SIGNAL
Please, Ultimate Supreme, sir, in no way is it our intention to make things difficult for you.
And we think we have a solution that would benefit everyone.
You are mucking up our operations and causing problems for me. Plus, you're annoying. So you must be exterminated at once. There is no alternative solution.
Dad, that's a little extreme, isn't it? Maybe we can just let them go. They're harmless.
Wow, son. When I said "try me," I didn't think you'd actually TRY ME.

So you're just going to let our planet die?
Maybe we can work something out?
We've got our own problems. You deal with yours.
But with all due respect, we are causing their problems, Ultimate Supreme, sir.
Oh yeah. You're right.
That's pretty deep, Karl. Ha!
But they are still annoying. Sentries! Ready your blasters!
Dad?
BEEP

ZOOOMM
WHOOOSHH!
SHOOM
SPIT
SPIT
SPIT
WHIRR
SPIT
FZZZT!
FZZZT
THUNK!
THUNK

Did you do that?
Yep.
Wow! You go, Blake Laser!
FZZZT
THUNK
BEEP!
ZAP
ZZAP
ZAP
POP!
Let's be reasonable here!
Don't move.

Karl? Zagbar? Aren't you going to stop them?
No, Dad. This could be good for everyone. Not just good for YOU!
My holo pad!
SCRIT SCRIT
Oh, you're mine now.
Mom, Dad—take this blue boogie down to the robot maintenance cell and guard him. I'm going to help Blake launch some rockets!

Maybe we can work something out?
When we asked you the same question earlier, you said no. Let's just stick with that.
You don't know who you're messin' with here.
Neither do you, blue boy.
SPLOOP
CHOMP

YANK
ZAP
What was that?
HEH HEH HEH!
TAP TAP TAP TAP

SHLOOP
Let's get these loaded up.

Okay. Everyone cross your fingers.
If you can.
BEEP!
LAUNCH
WHOOOSH
Wow, your rockets are fast.
They're courtesy of the Borsulons. They're designed to travel light-years. This distance is nothing.

TIME REMAINING TO TARGET 1 MIN 40 SEC
0 MIN 33 SEC
Hit it!
ARRIVED AT TARGET
Karl, on my mark, initiate the deployment sequence.
BEEP
CHK CHK
MISS

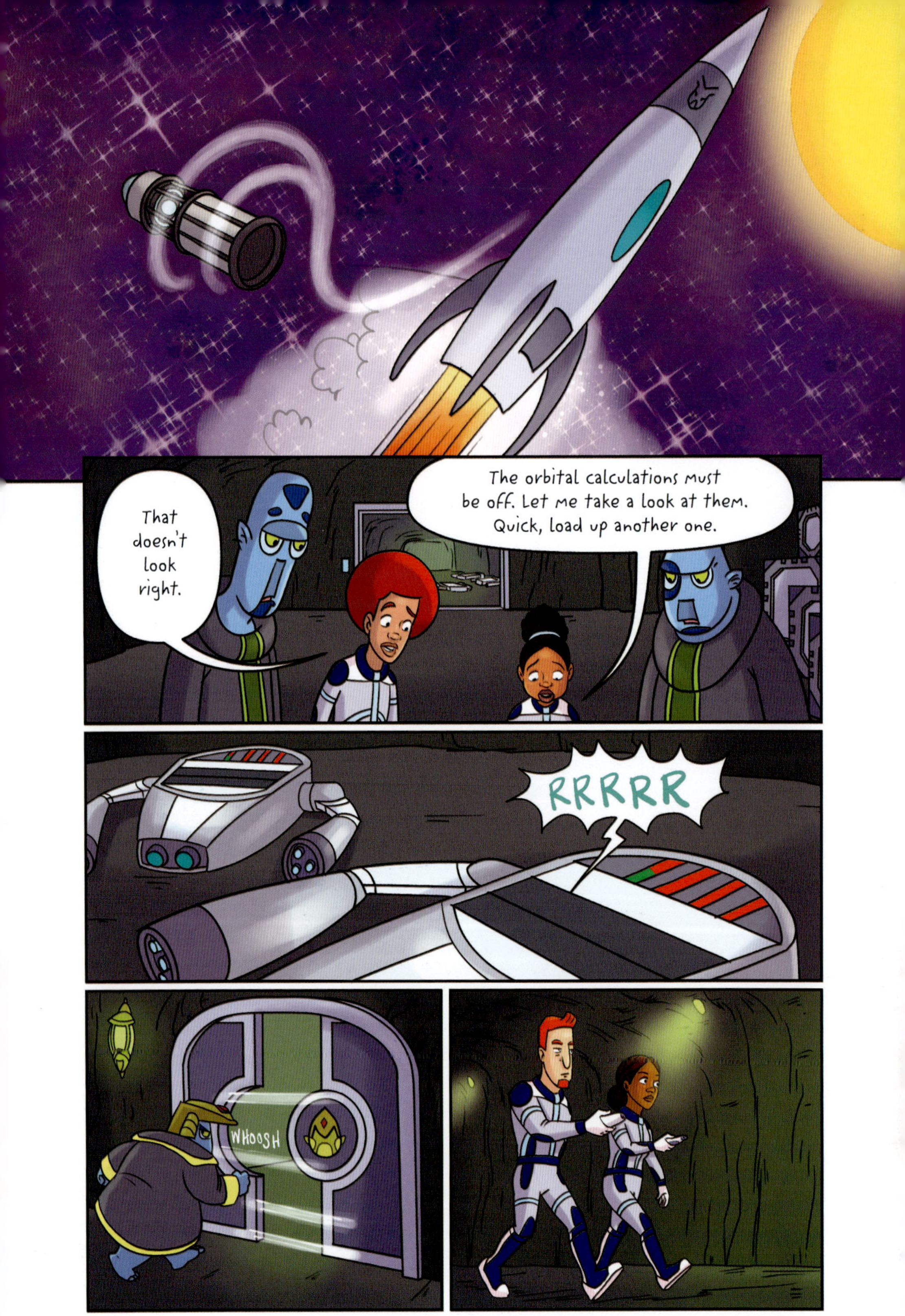
That doesn't look right.
The orbital calculations must be off. Let me take a look at them. Quick, load up another one.
RRRRR
WHOOSH

ZAAP
Nice try. Let's go.
I wonder what's taking so long? We'd better get back to the launch compound and see what's going on.
Right.
Ready!
Launch!
WHOOOSHH
TIME REMAINING TO TARGET
0 MIN 33 SEC

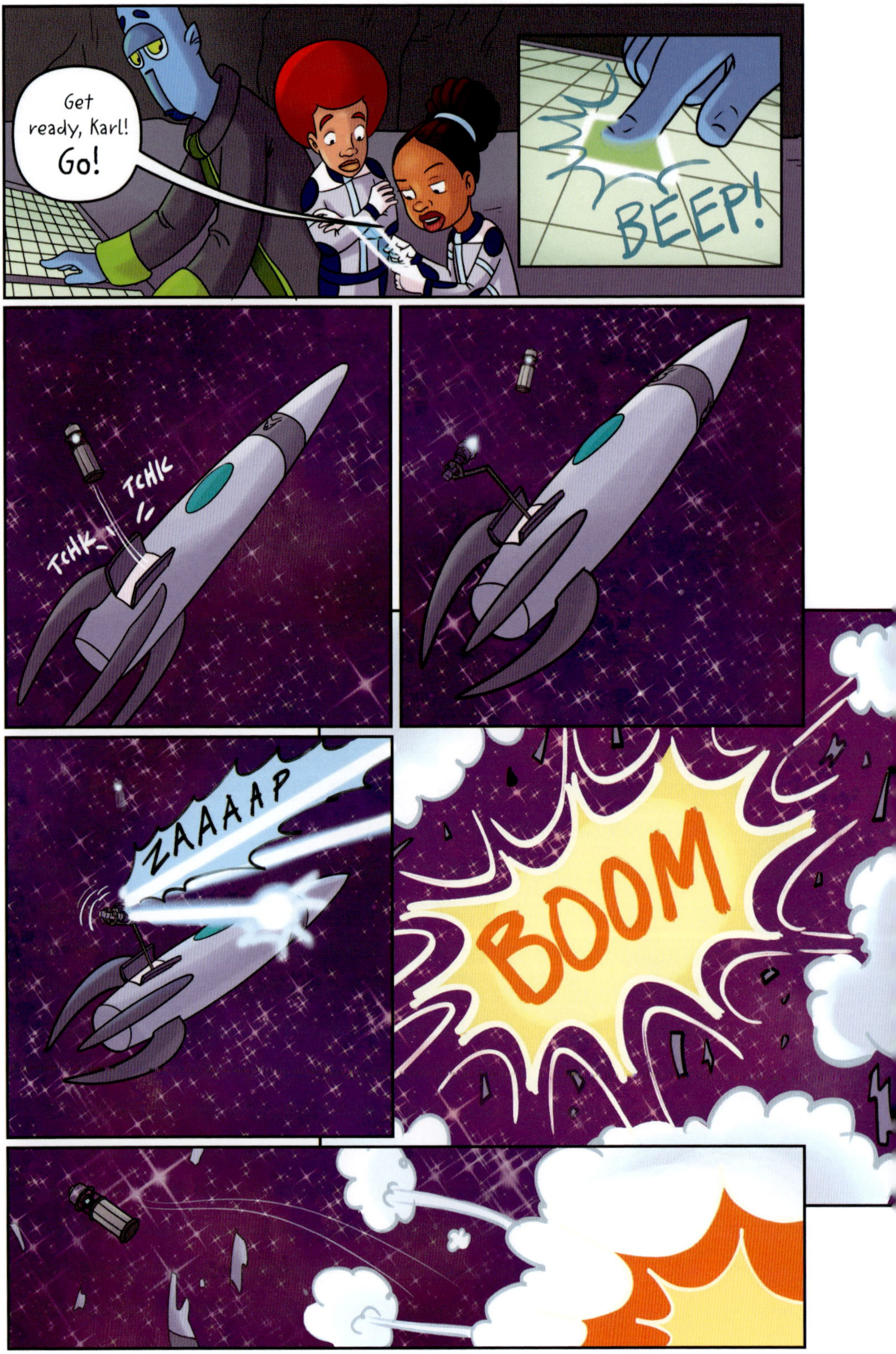
Get ready, Karl! Go!
BEEP!
TCHK
TCHK
ZAAAAP
BOOM

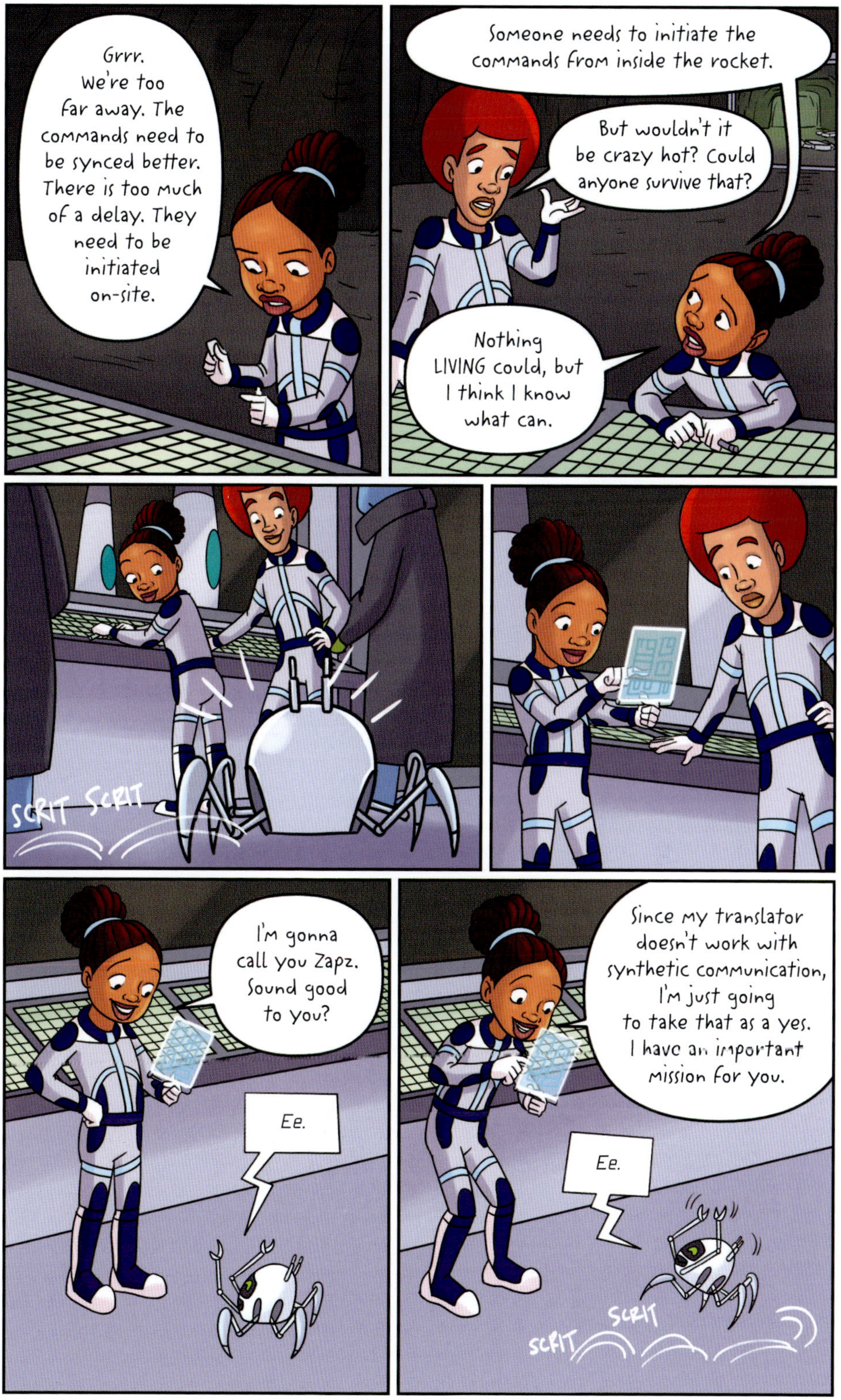
Grrr.
We're too far away. The commands need to be synced better. There is too much of a delay. They need to be initiated on-site.
Someone needs to initiate the commands from inside the rocket.
But wouldn't it be crazy hot? Could anyone survive that?
Nothing LIVING could, but I think I know what can.
SCRIT SCRIT
I'm gonna call you Zapz. Sound good to you?
Ee.
Since my translator doesn't work with synthetic communication, I'm just going to take that as a yes. I have an important mission for you.
Ee.
SCRIT SCRIT

RRRRRRRRRRRRRRRRRRRR
Our friends are waking up!
RRRRRRRRRRRRRRRRRR
Take this. It will link you with the communications in the rocket. I promise to bring you back in one piece. This is our last fancy lamp, and...
...you're our last hope.
HIGH FIVE!
SCRIT
SCRIT

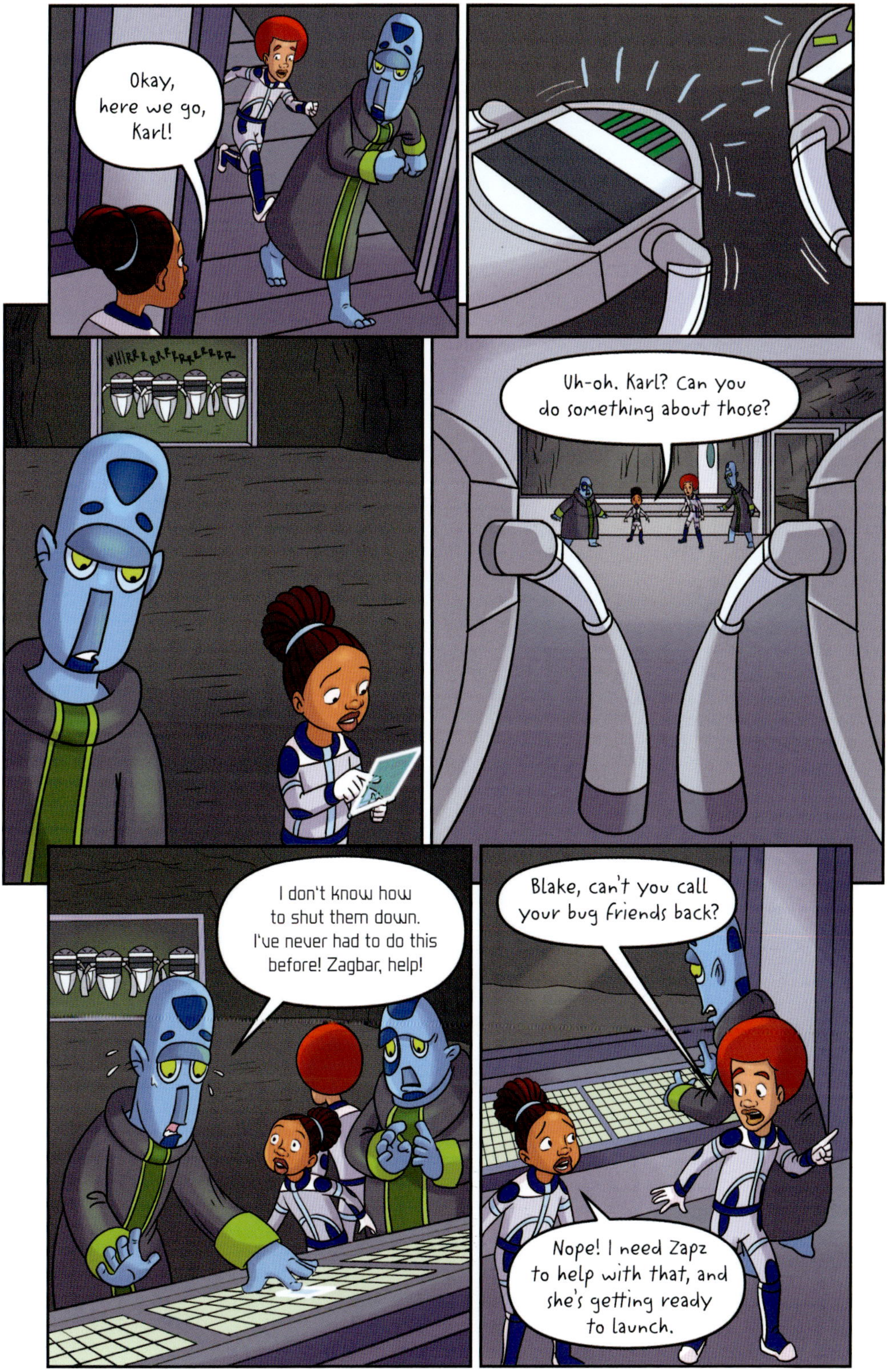
Okay, here we go, Karl!
WHIRRRRRRRRRRRRRRR
Uh-oh. Karl? Can you do something about those?
I don't know how to shut them down. I've never had to do this before! Zagbar, help!
Blake, can't you call your bug friends back?
Nope! I need Zapz to help with that, and she's getting ready to launch.

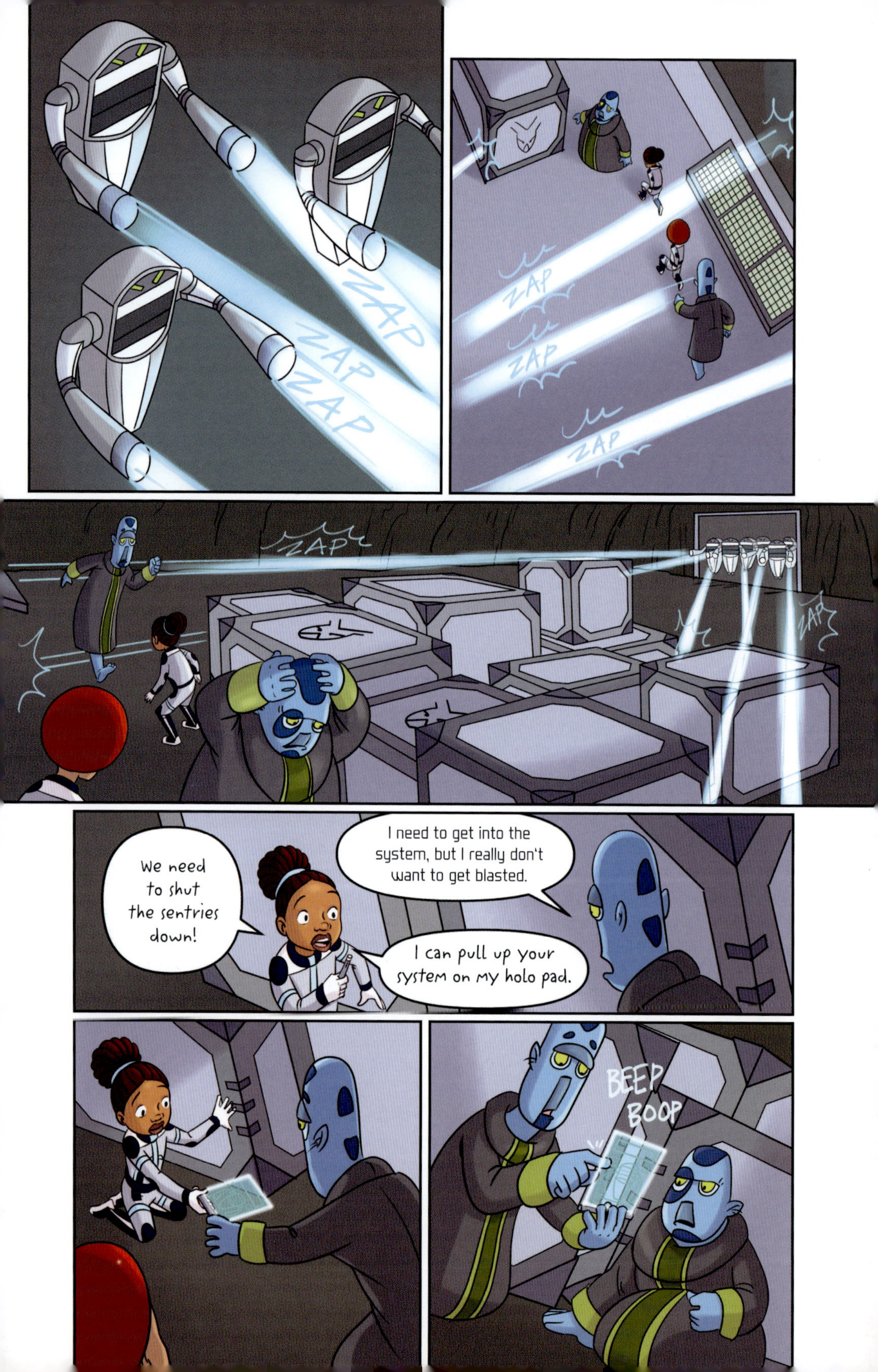
ZAP
ZAP
ZAP
ZAP
ZAP
ZAP
ZAP
ZAP
We need to shut the sentries down!
I need to get into the system, but I really don't want to get blasted.
I can pull up your system on my holo pad.
BEEP
BOOP

Hey, Zagbar! It's asking for a supervisor! I need you to press this button for me before the sentries kill us, okay?
THUNK
THUNK
YES! Thank you!
THANK YOU!

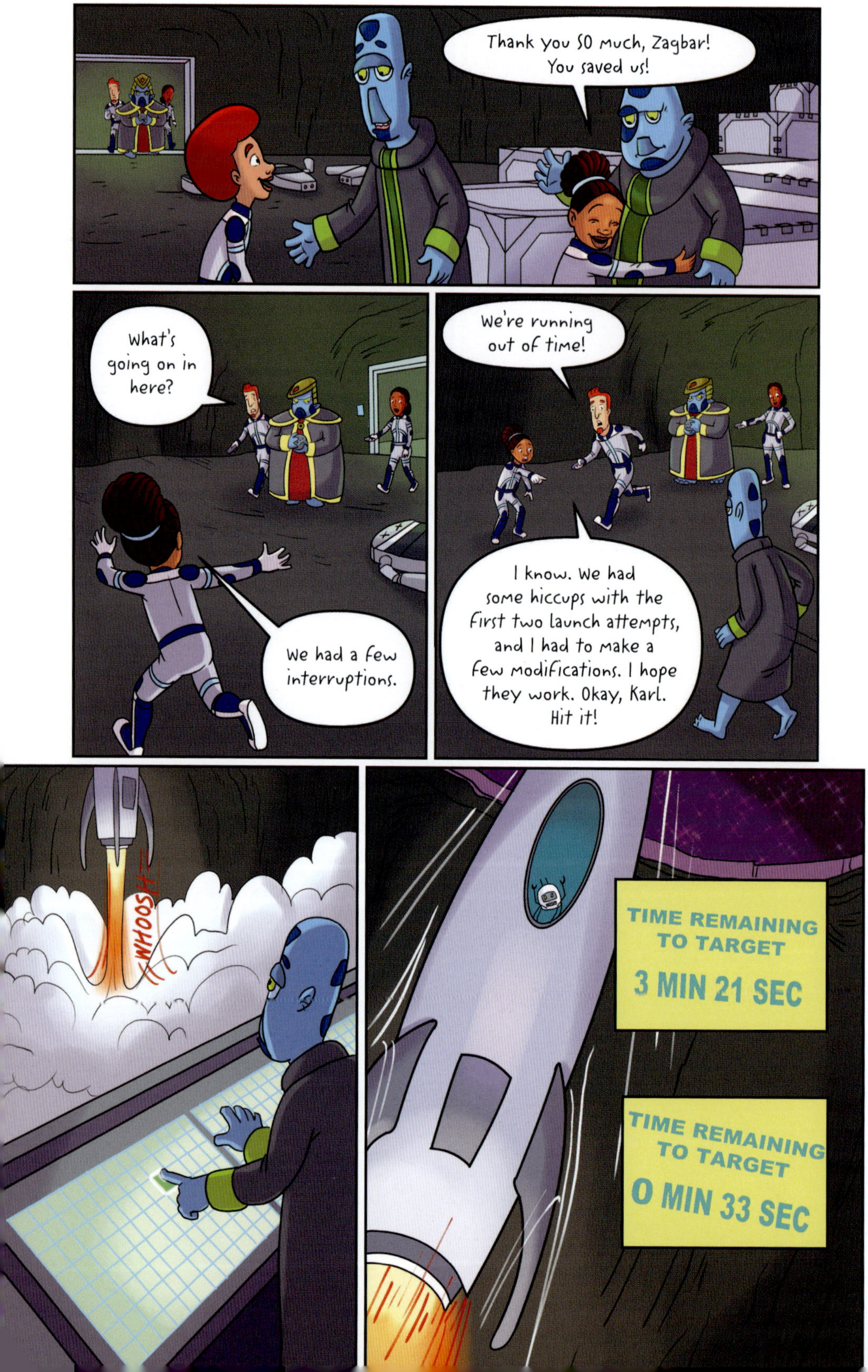
Thank you SO much, Zagbar! You saved us!
What's going on in here?
We had a few interruptions.
We're running out of time!
I know. We had some hiccups with the first two launch attempts, and I had to make a few modifications. I hope they work. Okay, Karl. Hit it!
WHOOSH
TIME REMAINING TO TARGET
3 MIN 21 SEC
TIME REMAINING TO TARGET
0 MIN 33 SEC

BEEP
BOOP
CLICK
BZZZZ
TCHK
TCHK
Come on!
Come on!
CLICK
TAP

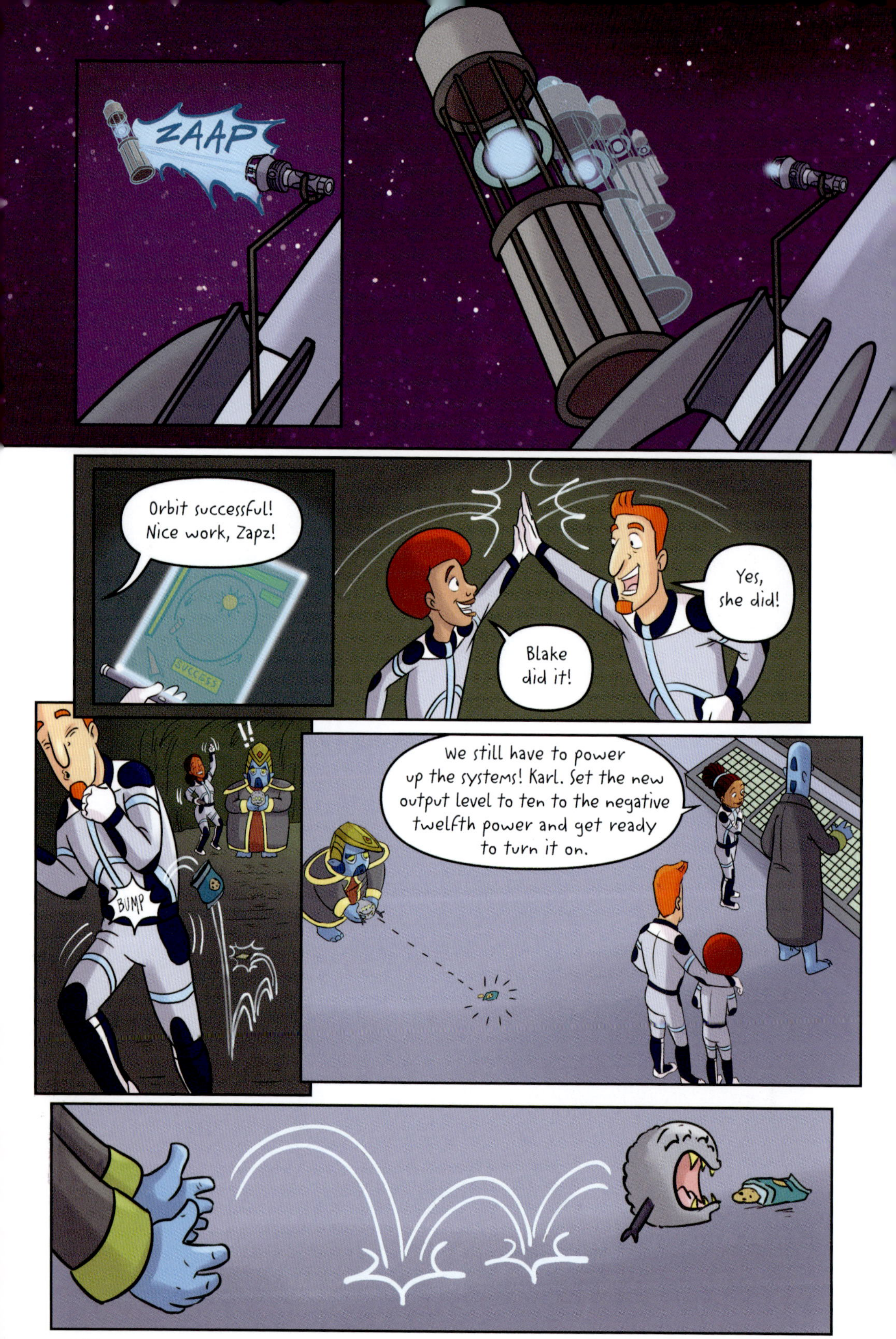
ZAAP
Orbit successful! Nice work, Zapz!
SUCCESS
Blake did it!
Yes, she did!
!!
BUMP
We still have to power up the systems! Karl. Set the new output level to ten to the negative twelfth power and get ready to turn it on.

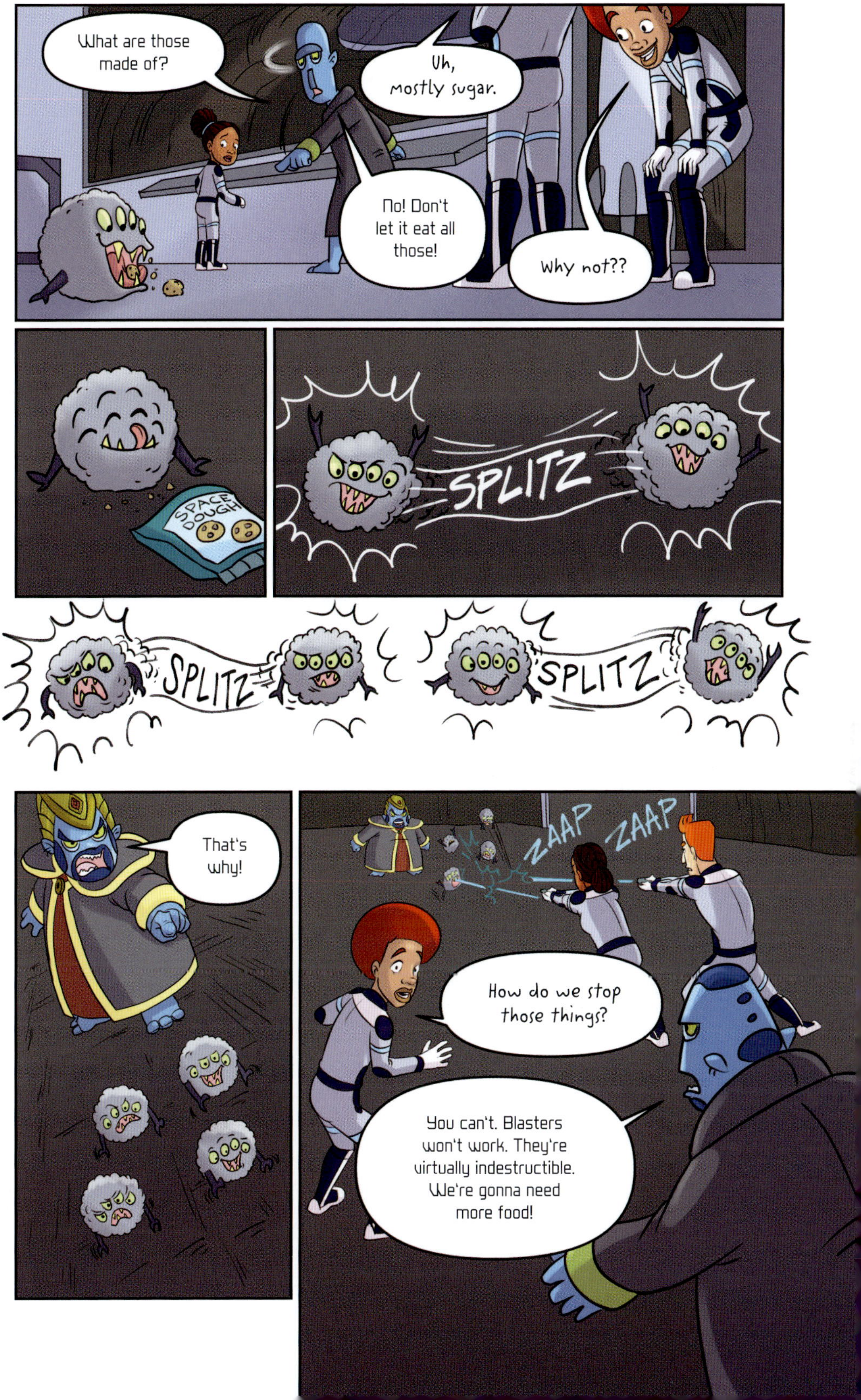
What are those made of?
Uh, mostly sugar.
No! Don't let it eat all those!
Why not??
SPACE DOUGH
SPLITZ
SPLITZ
SPLITZ
That's why!
ZAAP
ZAAP
How do we stop those things?
You can't. Blasters won't work. They're virtually indestructible. We're gonna need more food!

I got nuthin.
ZAAP
ZAAP
They won't stop, so we'll need to lure them away.
To where?
Out to the rockets! Help us with the launch!
Help your mom hold them off!
ZAP
ZAP
Show them the food and then toss it into the ship!

Toss it in now!!
I'm gonna miss you.
ZAAP
SLAM
WHOOOSH
Sayonara!

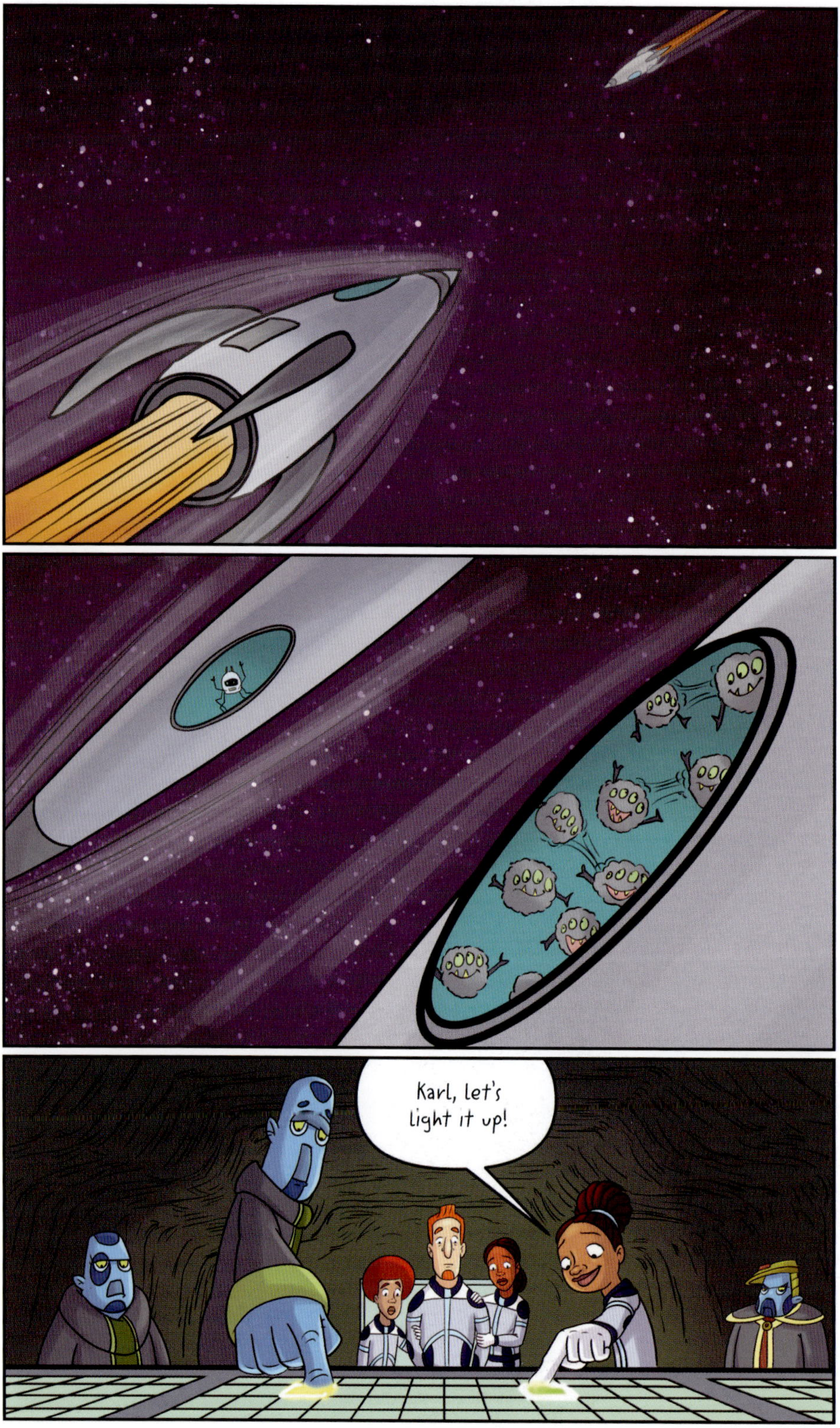
Karl, let's light it up!

IT'S WORKING!
NOW she did it!
BLAKE LAAAASERRRR!
Nice work, Blake.
Well done.

SCRIT
SCRIT
SCRIT
SCRIT
SCRIT
HIGH FIVE!
Great job, Zapz!
Okay, why don't you find a nice place to cool your circuits? You've earned it.
SCRIT
SCRIT
SCRIT
SCRIT

HUMPH
CALL INCOMING
BLIP
What in high helioid are you doing?
And I thought THEY looked freaky.

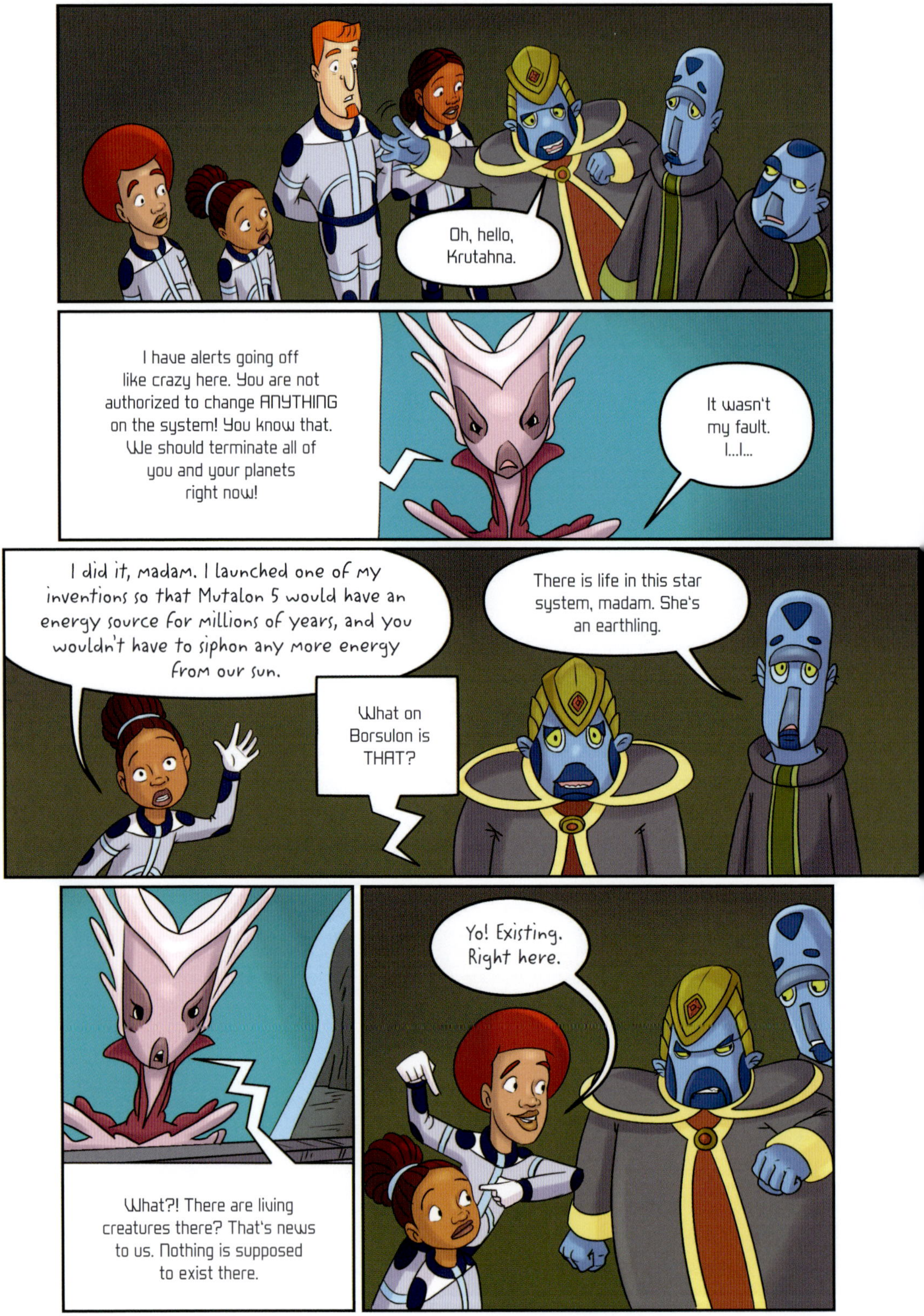
Oh, hello, Krutahna.
I have alerts going off like crazy here. You are not authorized to change ANYTHING on the system! You know that. We should terminate all of you and your planets right now!
It wasn't my fault. I...I...
I did it, madam. I launched one of my inventions so that Mutalon 5 would have an energy source for millions of years, and you wouldn't have to siphon any more energy from our sun.
What on Borsulon is THAT?
There is life in this star system, madam. She's an earthling.
What?! There are living creatures there? That's news to us. Nothing is supposed to exist there.
Yo! Existing. Right here.

I see. Well, all flagrant violations aside, I must admit that the system is working at a high efficiency rate. The output is remarkable. The supply level is off the charts. I've never seen a reading like that before.
Even though we no longer will have the Mutaloneon business, your system would be great for our profits elsewhere. We'll discuss that with you later.
Thank you, madam.
As for you, Flart, you'd best step up efforts with your mining production. You were slacking off quite a bit before this debacle.
I will see to it personally that Karl makes sure that production is satisfactory.
It'd better be. In the meantime, Hootoob from management wants you to call him for your performance review. Pronto!
Hmmm. And earthling?
Yes, madam?
Keep up the good work.
BLIP
WOOO-HOOOO!

I hate to break up the party, but it's time to go.
The hovers and the ship need to be repaired before we can get off this rock.
Thank you, Karl. That was a bold move, doing what you did to help us out.
It's a horrible feeling thinking your world is coming to an end.
That's something we have in common, but for us, we've felt that way for a long time. And since our stars are now connected, so are we.
Be well, Blake Laser.
You too!
Bye, Zagbar.
Goodbye.
And smile a little more, will you?
I packed up the tools. Please be extra careful with them.
Okay...?

Blake! For your heroic efforts and annoying persistence, I'd like to invite your family to Mutalon 5 at some point in the not too distant future. But not that soon either. We'll call you. Give Karl your digits. Karl, get her digits.
Thank you. I guess we'll be seeing you, then.
You never invite anyone to the planet.
Yeah, what gives?
Oh, I have plans for Blake Laser.
Big plans.

Chapter 11

A Pleasant Family Experience